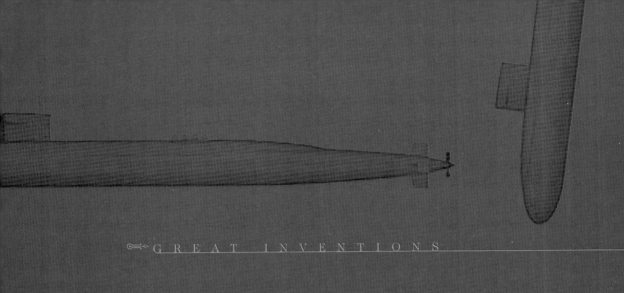

Submarines

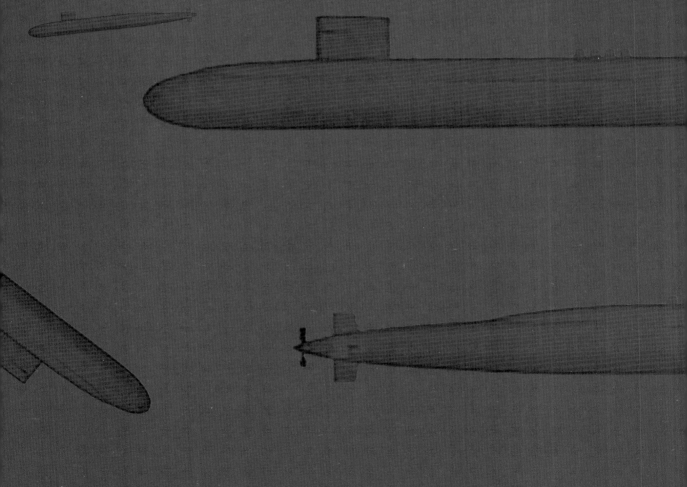

GREAT INVENTIONS

Submarines

REBECCA STEFOFF

Marshall Cavendish
Benchmark
New York

Marshall Cavendish Benchmark
99 White Plains Road
Tarrytown, NY 10591-9001
www.marshallcavendish.us

Library of Congress Cataloging-in-Publication Data

Stefoff, Rebecca, 1951–
Submarines / Rebecca Stefoff.
p. cm. — (Great inventions)
Summary: "An examination of the origin, history, development, and impact of the
submarine and related underwater exploration and transport technology"—Provided by publisher.
Includes bibliographical references and index.
ISBN-13: 978-0-7614-2229-7
ISBN-10: 0-7614-2229-3
1. Submarines (Ships)—Juvenile literature. 2. Submersibles—Juvenile
literature. I. Title. II. Series.

V857.S83 2006
623.825'7—dc22

2005033984

Series design by Sonia Chaghatzbanian

Photo research by Candlepants, Inc.

Cover photo: Getty Images/Brand X

The photographs in this book are used by permission and through the courtesy of: *Getty Images:*
Sandy Huffaker, 2; Hulton Archive, 34, 39, 54, 64, 72, 84, 88, 90, 93; 98. *Corbis:* Reuters, 8, 11, 13;
SYGMA, 14; 57, 76; Bettmann, 59, 70, 79; Hulton-Deutsch Collection, 74, 83; Horace Bristol, 78;
Roger Ressmeyer, 96; Toby Melville/Reuters, 104. *OAR/National Undersea Research Program:* 28.
chinfo.navy.mil.: 35. *Photo Researchers Inc.:* Alexis Rosenfeld, 101. *The Image Works:* The British
Library/HIP, 18; Mary Evans Picture Library, 24, 25, 30, 37, 40, 44–45, 46, 51, 53, 66, 68, 52–53,
106–107; SSPL, 27; SSPL/Science Museum, 43; Lebrecht, 62.

Printed in China
1 3 5 6 4 2

CONTENTS

Submarines

The Russian submarine *K-141*, or *Kursk*, at anchor in the Russian Arctic port of Vidyayevo in May 2000. The nuclear-powered *Kursk* was five years old at the time and was being equipped with new weapons.

The Dangerous World of the Submariner

The Barents Sea is always cold, even in August. Its gray waters stretch north from Scandinavia and western Russia to merge with the Arctic Ocean. This is the territory of Russia's northern fleet. From their home port of Murmansk, the ships and submarines of the fleet patrol the Barents Sea, sometimes carrying out military exercises there, practicing maneuvers and testing equipment. On Saturday, August 12, 2000, the Russian nuclear submarine *K-141* was about to perform such an exercise, which would include test-firing one of the boat's brand-new weapons. The 118 men aboard did not know how perilous that weapon would prove to be.

The Russian navy had fallen on hard times. Its nuclear submarine program, in particular, had been plagued for years with disasters and life-threatening accidents. One sub, *K-19,* had experienced a potentially deadly malfunction in its nuclear reaction core, then a collision with an American spy sub, and, a few years later, a devastating fire. Another, *K-219,* sank off the Atlantic island of Bermuda after an explosion and several later fires aboard. Then, in 1989, fire caused the sinking of the *Komsomolets* in the Norwegian Sea, claiming the lives of forty-two crewmen, some of whom perished in the brutally cold water after escaping from the sub. Conditions worsened during the 1990s, after the fall of the Soviet Union, the communist state that Russia had controlled for several generations. Russia's new democratic government, desperately short of funds, cut the country's military budget. By 2000 Russia was spending the equivalent of five billion dollars a year on all branches of its military, compared with about three hundred billion a year in military spending by the United States. As many as 180 Soviet-era nuclear subs had been decommissioned, or taken out of service, to lie rusting in dockyards and harbors. Maintenance and officer training for the submarines still in service had suffered. An American naval officer who knew of these potentially dangerous conditions called the Russian navy "an accident waiting to happen."

A key part of Russia's navy was the *Oscar* class of submarines, a category of large, nuclear-powered, missile-carrying boats. These subs were 505 feet (154 meters) across and almost 60 feet (18.3 meters) wide. They could carry and fire a variety of weapons, including surface-to-surface missiles with nuclear warheads. *K-141*, which had come into service in 1995, was an *Oscar*-class submarine. To commemorate the site of a Soviet victory in World War II, it had been dubbed *Kursk*, a name soon to be known around the world.

In preparation for the naval exercises of that August morning, the *Kursk* had been fitted with a new weapon: an array of rocket-propelled torpedoes. High-ranking Russian naval officers were aboard to observe the test-firing of one of the new torpedoes, as were several technicians from the factory that had made the torpedoes. Also observing—but from much farther away—were the American submarines *Toledo* and *Memphis*, which monitored and recorded the naval maneuvers as part of their surveillance mission in Russian waters. Such cat-and-mouse submarine games, with each side prowling along the other's coasts and shadowing the other's fleets, had been standard procedure since the mid-twentieth century.

Before testing the new torpedoes, the *Kursk* fired an unarmed version of one of its older weapons: a cruise missile that could be used to attack surface ships. *Oscar*-class submarines carry twenty-four such

LESS THAN A MONTH BEFORE THE *KURSK*'S FATEFUL ACCIDENT, THE CREW POSED ON DECK DURING A NAVAL PARADE IN THE RUSSIAN CITY OF SEVEROMORSK. COMMANDER GENNADI LYACHIN IS AT THE FAR RIGHT.

missiles in tubes outside their hulls. The *Kursk*'s cruise missile fired perfectly. Next, the launch crew and the command crew prepared to demonstrate the new torpedo, which was powered by a fuel called high-test hydrogen peroxide (HTP). Because HTP is highly flammable and explosive, the U.S. Navy had stopped using it thirty years earlier. HTP is also relatively inexpensive and quite powerful, however, which is why the Russians continued to use it. The crew of the *Kursk* knew that firing the torpedo would be extremely loud. To soften the impact of the sound, they opened the watertight doors between the sub's compartments—a fairly common practice, even though it violates safety regulations. Once everyone was ready, the *Kursk*'s captain, veteran submarine commander Gennadi Lyachin, gave the order to fire the torpedo.

And then things went horribly wrong. The rocket's HTP exploded, splitting open the torpedo and its tube. Seawater poured through the torpedo tube into the launch compartment, mixing with the roaring, fast-burning fuel. The burst of flame and water devoured the launch crew instantly, but it didn't stop there. It sped through the open hatchway, killing everyone it touched. Lyachin immediately ordered a blow, or emergency surfacing, but the sub did not rise. What happened next made the situation inside the sub even worse. The fire in the launch compartment reached a torpedo rack, causing at least one more torpedo to explode. It was as if several tons of TNT had exploded in a confined space. The explosion was strong enough to register on seismographs, or earthquake-recording devices, across northern Europe. It punched an enormous hole through the *Kursk's* bow, and the sea rushed in. Within seconds, everyone in the front two-thirds of the *Kursk,* including everyone in the control room, was dead. The boat plunged down and struck the bottom of the Barents Sea at a depth of about 350 feet (93 meters).

On the surface, confusion swirled in the aftermath of the disaster. The Russian government waited for two days before publicly announcing the sinking of the *Kursk,* then claimed that the accident had occurred a day later than it really did. When word reached the public that Russian rescue vessels reported knocking or tapping sounds coming from inside the sunken sub, possibly made by survivors, several foreign navies offered to help with rescue attempts. Russia's leaders delayed in accepting these offers. By the time rescue units from Great Britain and Norway arrived on the scene, four days after the accident, there was little or no hope of finding survivors alive.

At first, rumors flew about the cause of the accident. According to some theories, the *Kursk* had been damaged in a collision with another submarine, probably the *Toledo.* Or perhaps the *Memphis* had fired on it by mistake. Other supposed explanations claimed that the *Kursk* had been accidentally struck by a friendly-fire torpedo launched from a nearby Russian surface ship during the military exercises. But after part of the *Kursk* was recovered in 2001, examination of the wreck, together with a review of the sound recordings made by the *Memphis,* revealed the sequence of events that most likely killed the *Kursk* and her crew.

Twenty-three crew members survived the initial blasts aboard the *Kursk* and the sinking of the submarine. They were in the stern, or rear third of the boat, separated from the broken front part of the hull by thick walls that shielded the sub's nuclear reactor. Because the *Kursk* had lost power, the survivors had no light and no heat. The water was rising around them, and the limited air supply was fouled by gas leaks or by carbon dioxide produced by the fire. Some of the men fumbled with pencils and paper, writing notes. At 3:45 in the afternoon, about four hours after the accident, Lieutenant Dmitry Kolesnikov wrote, "It's too dark to write, but I'll try by touch. It seems there is little chance, 10-20 percent. At least I hope someone will read this. . . . Mustn't despair." Although the full truth of the survivors' ordeal will probably never be known, experts who have studied the case think that some of them could have remained alive for a day, perhaps two. They died of asphyxiation, or lack of oxygen, before rescue was possible.

DEEP SUBMERGENCE RESCUE VEHICLES (DSRVS) LIKE THIS ONE ARE RUSHED TO THE SCENE WHEN A TRAGEDY SUCH AS THE SINKING OF THE *KURSK* TAKES PLACE. OCCASIONALLY, THOUGH, EVEN THE RESCUE VEHICLES NEED TO BE RESCUED.

The *Kursk* made headlines around the world, but it was not alone. Submarine disasters and misadventures filled the news in the early years of the twenty-first century. In 2001 the U.S. Navy submarine *Greeneville* accidentally collided with a Japanese ship, the *Ehime Maru,* that was being used as a training vessel for commercial fishing workers and had several students aboard. The accident took place near the Hawaiian island of Oahu while the *Greeneville* was practicing an emergency surfacing drill. Nine Japanese died. A naval review later concluded that the captain and crew had not adequately scanned the area. The following year, the USS *Dolphin* flooded and caught fire off the California coast. After its crew abandoned the submarine, they were rescued. But the seventy crew members of China's *Ming 362* submarine were less fortunate. All died in 2003 in a mechanical malfunction—possibly a problem that caused the diesel engines to burn up all of the oxygen. That same year, the Russian *K-159,* a decommissioned submarine that was being towed to a scrap yard, sank in the Barents Sea. Of the ten crewmen aboard the sub, nine drowned. Still other accident scenarios unfolded. In 2004 a pair of fires aboard the Canadian sub *Chicoutimi* killed one crew member and damaged the boat. The following year, one man died and dozens were seriously injured when the USS *San Francisco* rammed an undersea mountain in the Pacific Ocean in the vicinity of the island of Guam. The collision, which destroyed the bow, or front, of the submarine, was caused by sloppy navigation techniques.

When the *Kursk* sank, one of the Russian ships that tried to come to its aid was carrying two DSRVs, or deep submergence rescue vehicles, of Russia's *Priz* class. These are 44-foot-long (13.4-meter-long) mini-submarines suitable for rescue and salvage work. One of the DSRVs was unusable. The other succeeded in reaching the sealed rear compartment of the *Kursk* but was unable to get a watertight seal on the hull, so it could not aid the crippled sub. Five years later, in August 2005, another *Priz*-class DSRV found itself in desperate need of rescue. *AS-28* was submerged off the Kamchatka Peninsula on Russia's east coast, carrying out a military mission that may have involved laying cables and sensors for an anti-submarine detection system on the seafloor. The mini-sub got tangled in something—some accounts say it was snarled in cables from the anti-sub system, others that it was caught in discarded fishing nets. Once entangled, *AS-28* was stuck at 600 feet (183 meters), too great a depth for the seven men aboard to swim to the surface in protective gear. Once again, Russia was unable to rescue its submarine, but this time the Russian government accepted foreign offers of help. First on the scene were British naval technicians, who flew to the nearest seaport with an unmanned remotely operated vehicle (ROV) called a Scorpio. A Russian ship then carried them to a position just above the sunken *AS-28*. The technicians launched the Scorpio and controlled it from the surface, directing its movable arms to cut away the entanglements. Finally free, *AS-28* rose to the surface, its crew alive and healthy after several suspense-filled days.

Explosion, fire, flood, asphyxiation, collision—with all that can go wrong below the surface of the sea, why would anyone want to go there? For several thousand years, people dreamed of traveling underwater. Some of them did it, or at least tried to. Their reasons for going into the deep fall into three categories: war, money, and curiosity.

The military motive is ancient. Long before the modern era, naval warriors realized that the ability to move secretly beneath the sea's surface, hidden from view, would give them a great advantage in attacking their enemies and defending their own ships or seaports. The financial motive also inspired early inventors. Some of the first ancestors of the submarine were built by entrepreneurs who hoped to salvage treasure or other goods from sunken ships. Marine salvage remains big business today, and modern commerical enterprises such as oil drilling, laying undersea telecommunications cables, and even submarine tourism also depend on submarines and their relatives—submersibles and ROVs or remotely operated vehicles. As for curiosity, some inventors and marine explorers were driven by the desire to explore the hidden depths of the undersea world. Today, mini-subs and other undersea craft are helping scientists learn more about what goes on in the water that covers almost 71 percent of the earth's surface.

The military motive is the first for which we have a written record—even if the record is not entirely reliable. An ancient text known as the *Problemata,* possibly written by the Greek philosopher Aristotle, claims that a former pupil of Aristotle—now known as Alexander the Great—ventured beneath the waves in 332 B.C.E., while his ships were besieging the city of Tyre in the eastern Mediterranean. Enemy divers swam underwater to cut the anchor ropes of Alexander's ships, after which the ships drifted and crashed into one another and the shore. Supposedly Alexander, intent on seeing for himself what was happening below the waterline, had himself lowered into the harbor inside a large glass jar or bell filled with air and spent some minutes there, afterward describing the sights he had seen. Centuries later, Alexander's undersea adventure was a popular subject for medieval illustrators, but there is no proof that it ever happened. Clearly, though, the principle of the diving bell—a container of air that allows a diver to breathe underwater for a short while—was known to people in the ancient world.

In the thirteenth century, the English scientist Roger Bacon touched on the financial motive for undersea ventures when he wrote of a device that allowed "labourers upon wrecks" to do salvage work underwater. Bacon described a kind of diving bell, an open-bottomed container that, when lowered into the water, would hold a bubble of air. Divers could work nearby, holding their breath, and swim or walk into the bell when they needed to breathe. Even before Bacon described a diving bell, something resembling a submarine had been described in the twelfth-century German poem *Salman and Morolf,* in which one of the characters spends two weeks on the bottom of the sea in a specially built leather boat, breathing through a tube. Morolf's diving boat was fictional, but the time was not far off when inventors would build and test real underwater machines.

luy auoit faitte. gul estoit   lams sauf descendu a terre

DID ALEXANDER THE GREAT REALLY GO BENEATH THE WAVES IN AN ANCIENT DIVING BELL? ALTHOUGH ALEXANDER WAS A BOLD SPIRIT, MODERN SCHOLARS THINK IT HIGHLY UNLIKELY THAT THIS PARTICULAR ADVENTURE TOOK PLACE. STILL, THE TALE SERVES AS A STARTING POINT FOR THE HISTORY OF SPECULATION ABOUT UNDERWATER TRAVEL.

The sketches and notes of one of history's most ingenious inventors, the Italian artist and engineer Leonardo da Vinci (1452–1519), show that he gave some thought to the challenges of undersea survival and travel. Leonardo claimed to have figured out how a person could remain underwater for an extended period of time, but he also declared that he would not publish the details of his method "because of the evil nature of men who practice assassination at the bottom of the sea." Modern scholars don't know exactly what Leonardo meant by that remark, but he must have feared that a device for traveling underwater would be used for deadly purposes. If Leonardo saw one of today's hunter-killer submarines, sleek undersea boats designed to attack ships, other subs, and targets on land, he might feel that his fears were justified. These submarines are the product of a long, slow process of trial and error that began less than sixty years after Leonardo's death.

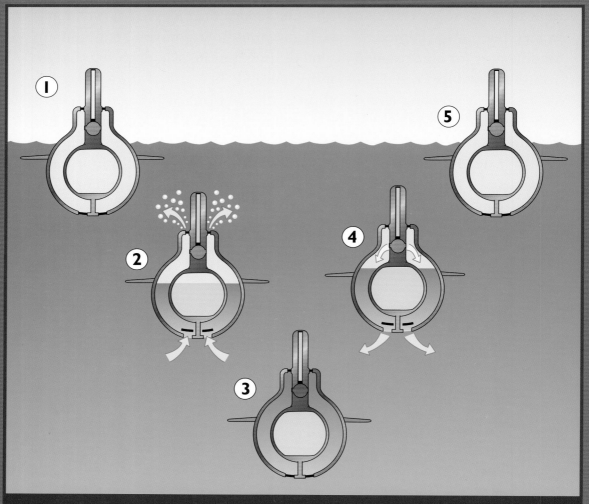

1. A SUBMARINE FILLED WITH AIR IS LESS DENSE THAN WATER. IT IS BUOYANT, FLOATING ON THE SURFACE.
2. SUBMARINES NEED BALLAST TO OVERCOME BUOYANCY. AS AIR LEAVES THE BALLAST TANKS, SEAWATER
RISES IN THEM. THE SUB LOSES BUOYANCY AND SINKS. 3. THE SUB'S VOLUME EQUALS THAT OF THE WATER
IT DISPLACES. THE SUB IS NEUTRALLY BUOYANT, NEITHER RISING NOR SINKING. 4. COMPRESSED AIR
BLOWN INTO THE BALLAST TANKS FORCES WATER OUT. THE SUB BECOMES POSITIVELY BUOYANT AND RISES.
5. WITH BALLAST TANKS EMPTY, THE SUB FLOATS AGAIN.

Early Undersea Ventures

In 1578 an Englishman named William Bourne published a book called *Inventions and Devices,* full of ideas, speculations, and descriptions of things that might someday be invented. One of Bourne's proposed "inventions" was "a shippe or boat that may goe under the water unto the bottom, and so come up again at your pleasure." Although Bourne produced neither a drawing nor a model of his undersea craft, his plan contained several important elements that all future submarine designers would have to consider.

Since ancient times engineers had understood the principle of displacement, which says that a body placed in water will displace a volume of water equal to its weight. Bourne, however, was the first to use that principle to explain why a boat floats—and how someone could make the boat sink and rise again. A boat floats on the surface by displacing a volume of water that equals its weight. If the boat displaced a lesser volume of water, it would sink; if it displaced a greater volume of water, it would rise. Bourne's plan was to cover a wooden rowboat with a leather covering treated with oil to make it waterproof. Inside the boat would be screws for alternately tightening and loosening parts of the leather covering. Winding in the leather would shrink the overall volume of the craft, reducing its displacement and causing it to sink. Winding out the leather would enlarge the volume of the craft, increasing its displacement and causing it to rise. Bourne also specified that a tall mast with a hole bored through the length of it should stick up through the cover. When the operator was ready to submerge the boat, he would check "the deepness of the water" and be careful not to let the top of the mast go below the surface, "for the hole that goeth through the mast must give you ayre, as men cannot live without it."

Bourne had come up with solutions to two challenges faced by any submarine designer: buoyancy (making the sub rise and sink on command) and air supply. A third challenge was propulsion, or making the craft move underwater. Cornelis Drebbel met that challenge in the early 1620s, when he built the first known working underwater boat.

Drebbel was a Dutch doctor who lived and worked in England, where King James I had named him "court inventor." Drebbel had many research interests, including bomb-building and alchemy. Turning his attention to submarine travel, he speculated that rowers propelling a boat across the water's surface might also be able to drive it beneath the surface, if the boat were properly designed and ballasted. Drebbel made his idea a reality, overseeing the building of at least one craft, possibly three or more. Because no drawings or plans from Drebbel's own time survive, marine historians use scattered references in letters and other sources to piece together a likely picture of his submarine. Drebbel seems to have begun with something like Bourne's idea—a wooden fishing boat topped by a framework of timbers and covered with a skin of oiled leather. Twelve rowers propelled the boat, using oars that passed through holes in the leather skin. Metal straps held the leather tight around the oars to prevent leaks. The most important feature of the boat's design was its angled front. The top of the boat sloped steeply toward the water in front, so that if the rowers pushed hard enough to build up speed, they would drive the bow not just forward but downward as well. As long as the rowers maintained their momentum, the pressure of the water on the bow would keep the boat down. All they had to do to make it rise was stop rowing. Modern experts think that the boat was probably weighted so that it floated barely above the surface when it was at rest. Rowed at top speed, it may have reached depths of 12 to 15 feet (3.7 to 4.6 meters). Londoners were amazed and delighted by demonstrations of Drebbel's submarine in the Thames River. Among those who admired the unusual craft were writer Ben Jonson, who called the contraption Drebbel's "invisible eel," and the inventor's patron King James, who probably paid for its construction. One account even suggests that the king took a ride in the boat, but modern historians think this claim is probably false—the king was well known to shrink from any physical risk.

The most surprising thing about Drebbel's success is that it did not inspire a host of immediate imitators. In the hundred years after Drebbel's invisible eel first took to the water, only two experimenters, both French, are known to have built submersible craft. The first builder, known only as De Son, created an underwater warship in 1653. Called the Rotterdam boat because De Son constructed it in that port city, now part of the Netherlands, this craft was built for Belgium to use against the English navy. It was not a true submarine because it was not meant to travel completely beneath the surface. Instead, it would move through the water awash, or almost submerged; the only thing showing above the surface would be a low deck with an opening to admit air and let the navigator see where the boat was going. The 72-foot-long (22-meter-long) wooden craft, shaped like a box with pointed ends, was designed as a stealth attack vessel. A large wooden beam, reinforced with metal, ran through its length. This beam was the boat's weapon—a ram with which to strike enemy ships, holing and sinking them. The ambitious De Son boasted that the boat would sink a hundred ships in a day. Traveling beneath the waves, where "no fire, nor Storm, or Bullets" could harm it, it would travel from Rotterdam to London and back in a day and to India in six weeks. De Son had drastically underestimated the amount of power needed to move his long, heavy vessel through the water, however. Intended to be driven by a clockwork arrangement of

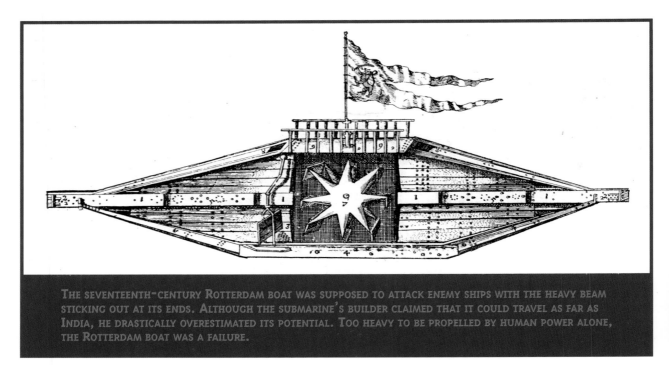

THE SEVENTEENTH-CENTURY ROTTERDAM BOAT WAS SUPPOSED TO ATTACK ENEMY SHIPS WITH THE HEAVY BEAM STICKING OUT AT ITS ENDS. ALTHOUGH THE SUBMARINE'S BUILDER CLAIMED THAT IT COULD TRAVEL AS FAR AS INDIA, HE DRASTICALLY OVERESTIMATED ITS POTENTIAL. TOO HEAVY TO BE PROPELLED BY HUMAN POWER ALONE, THE ROTTERDAM BOAT WAS A FAILURE.

springs and paddlewheels, the Rotterdam boat went nowhere. It did not function and was never used.

Although De Son's fiasco was the only underwater boat attempted in the years following Drebbel, submarines were on people's minds. In 1648 an Englishman named John Wilkins had published a work called *Mathematicall Magick.* In it he listed the potential advantages of an undersea vessel: secrecy; safety from storms, pirates, ice, and other surface dangers; and military uses, such as surprise attacks, destruction of enemy ships from beneath, and the smuggling of supplies to besieged ports. A final advantage was that an undersea craft would open up the possibility of scientific discovery. However, Wilkins, who later became a bishop, was not a practical experimenter. Although he foresaw the submarine's role in military strategy, he never actually tried to build one.

Another theorist, Giovanno Borelli of Italy, published his own list of inventions and devices in 1680. One device he sketched was a wooden submarine boat. Borelli tackled the problem of water displacement with a unique ballast system—a set of goatskin bags that would alter the boat's weight, not its size. The operator would submerge the boat by allowing the bags to fill with water. To surface, he would have to squeeze the water out of the bags. Borelli didn't build his proposed submarine, which was a stroke of good luck for him. The boat would most likely have sunk, but it probably would not have risen. A decade later, French mathematician Denis Papin reportedly built a submarine and started work on a second. Little is known about his design, which used an air pump to control the vessel's buoyancy. Papin abandoned work when his financial backer stopped supplying funds.

Money problems cut short the experiments of another early submariner, English carpenter Nathaniel Symons. In 1729 Symons built a submarine that resembled the one Bourne had described. It was a covered

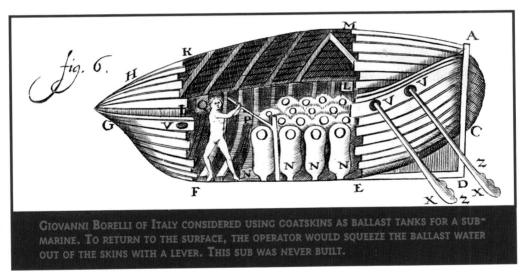

GIOVANNI BORELLI OF ITALY CONSIDERED USING GOATSKINS AS BALLAST TANKS FOR A SUBMARINE. TO RETURN TO THE SURFACE, THE OPERATOR WOULD SQUEEZE THE BALLAST WATER OUT OF THE SKINS WITH A LEVER. THIS SUB WAS NEVER BUILT.

wooden boat in two sections, joined by a panel of accordion-pleated leather that could fold and unfold. Sitting inside, Symons turned screws to pull the two wooden sections together or spread them apart again. As the boat grew smaller and then larger, it sank and then rose. Because Symons's boat had no means of propulsion, all he could do was go underwater and come up again, but that in itself was a remarkable achievement. Symons demonstrated his boat in the River Dart in south-eastern England, once spending three-quarters of an hour beneath the surface. He hoped that the people who flocked to watch his amazing feats would pay for their entertainment, but his collections never amounted to more than small change, so Symons abandoned his boat and his project, even though he had developed a functional submersible craft.

The submarine made a second appearance as a money-making stunt in 1774. This time, the luckless submariner suffered more than discouragement. He was an English wheelwright named John Day, who had already made one submersible craft by constructing a watertight cabin in the middle of a small boat. Once he was inside the floating cabin, helpers hung heavy stones on the outside to serve as ballast, weighting the boat so it would sink. The stones were attached by bolts that Day could release from inside the boat when he wanted to return to the surface. Day tested this craft in 30 feet (9 meters) of water and later claimed to have spent twenty-four hours beneath the surface. That may have been an exaggeration, but the success of the first venture gave Day the confidence to take a professional gambler named Christopher Blake as his partner. Blake bought a larger boat and paid to have it converted into a watertight submersible. Day announced publicly that he would enter this boat and descend to the bottom of Plymouth Harbor, about 100 feet (30 meters) down. After twelve hours, he would rise to the surface unharmed. Betting that Day would succeed, Blake made wagers with a number of doubters. The deal was that Blake would give Day 10 percent of his winnings. When the great day came, Day stocked his cabin with a hammock, a candle, biscuits, and water. His helpers attached the ballast, and Day's submersible sank like a stone. What Day had not realized is that although his tightly sealed vessel could withstand the pressure of water at 30 feet (9 meters) down, the pressure at 100 feet (30 meters) would be enough to crumple it like tinfoil. Neither Day nor his boat was seen again.

Despite Day's crushing failure, inventors persisted. Just two years after Day disappeared in Plymouth Harbor, one innovator built the first submarine ever used to attack an enemy ship. In the summer of 1776,

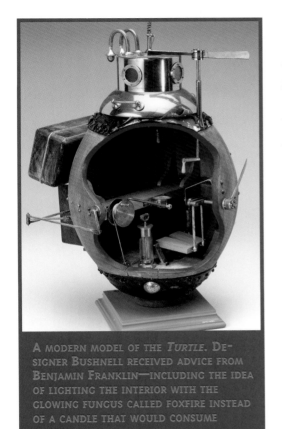

at the beginning of the American fight for independence from Great Britain, a colonist named David Bushnell put his long-time interest in underwater inventions to practical use. His goal was to attack British warships that were blockading colonial ports. First Bushnell invented an underwater mine—a 150-pound (68-kilogram) keg of gunpowder that could be set to explode with a clockwork timer. Then, with advice from Benjamin Franklin and encouragement (and funds) from George Washington, he produced a small, stealthy craft to deliver the mine to its target. Bushnell's craft was called the *Turtle* because it looked like a big sea turtle floating vertically in the water. Although no drawings from Bushnell's time exist, we know that the *Turtle* was egg-shaped, with a weighted bottom to keep it steady. It held one person, who entered through a watertight hatch in the top. Air tubes provided ventilation and closed automatically when the *Turtle* submerged, leaving the operator with about half an hour's worth of air. The operator raised and lowered the *Turtle* by using a foot pedal that controlled a valve. When the valve let water in, the *Turtle* submerged. When it forced the water out again, the *Turtle* surfaced.

The *Turtle* was designed to be a true submarine—a vessel that could navigate independently both on the surface and completely submerged. Yet it could not have been easy to use. Its only source of power was the operator. In addition to regulating depth with the foot pedal, peering through a small viewport or examining a compass to navigate, and steering with a hand-operated rudder that controlled the *Turtle*'s direction, the operator turned two hand cranks to control the propellers that

Connecticut colonist David Bushnell built the Revolutionary War submarine the *Turtle*. Although the Americans hoped to use the *Turtle* against British ships blockading New York harbor, the submarine's sole mission ended in failure.

moved the craft through the water. One crank operated a propeller that moved the *Turtle* forward or backward; the other operated a second propeller that moved it up or down. Getting around in the *Turtle* required feats of strength and stamina, but the craft was not intended to travel long distances. The plan was to tow it to the general area of its target, then send it beneath the surface to complete its mission. When the *Turtle* reached its target, its operator would have to perform even more tasks—drilling a screw into the hull of the enemy ship, transferring the mine from the outside of the *Turtle* to the screw, and arming the clockwork timer, all the while keeping his submarine steady. Then, of course, the pilot would have to get the *Turtle* to a safe distance before the mine exploded.

Was the *Turtle* usable? The physical demands of operating it "would have tested the dexterity of a trained octopus," according to military historian Thomas Parrish, author of *The Submarine: A History* (2004). Inventor Bushnell was not up to the task, so Sergeant Ezra Lee of the colonial army volunteered. After Bushnell had trained Lee in the submarine's operation, the sergeant set off from lower Manhattan Island on his historic mission on the night of September 6, 1776. His target was the *Eagle,* a British flagship anchored off Staten Island.

Accounts differ as to exactly what happened next. One thing all agree on is that the *Turtle* did not accomplish its mission: the *Eagle* didn't explode. Lee later claimed to have reached the *Eagle* after losing some time battling the tide, but he said that the drill failed to penetrate the ship's hull. So historians have suggested that he may have tried to attach the mine at a point where the wooden hull was reinforced with a metal strip that supported the ship's rudder. Others have speculated that Lee, breathing inside a small sealed compartment, may have suffered from carbon-dioxide poisoning, which could have left him weak and confused. Whatever the case, when dawn approached Lee decided to retreat. During its withdrawal, the *Turtle* was not submerged. It was awash—that is, just barely breaking the surface, probably so that Lee could breathe and see more easily. According to some versions of the story, the English spotted the bizarre object moving through the water and gave chase in rowboats, and Lee released the mine to distract them. At any rate, he returned safely to shore, but the *Turtle*'s first voyage was also its last. It was simply too hard to use to be effective.

The next submarine, also built by an American, also failed to be practical because it was difficult to use. The builder was Robert Fulton, an artist turned inventor who at the end of the eighteenth century spent many years in Europe, first in England and then in France. Fulton came to hate the British navy. He was of Irish descent and resented Great Britain's treatment of Ireland. He also sympathized with the ideals of the French revolutionary government and sided with France in its ongoing conflict with Britain. Fulton felt that Britain was using its navy, at the time the world's most powerful seagoing force, to strangle liberty and prevent free trade around the world. Turning his mind to naval warfare, he considered how to take on such a mighty navy. The answer, he decided, was the submarine. By the late 1790s he had developed a design for an undersea boat that he called the *Nautilus*. Others had developed primitive versions of "plunging boats," as some called them, but Fulton intended to make the submarine into the ultimate weapon. He also intended to turn a profit. Fulton approached the French government and offered to build a submarine that could sink British ships with mines—if the French would pay him a bounty for every ship he sank.

Fulton's offer raised questions about the proper conduct of war. Would something as stealthy as a submarine attack violate the rules of combat that "civilized" nations liked to think they followed? Would the world condemn submarine attacks as cowardly and underhanded? Fulton was afraid that it would. He wanted the French government to make him and his submarine crew officers in the French navy, so that if they were captured by the enemy they would not be executed as pirates. But although Fulton worried about how the world would view submarine warfare, he also argued that submarines could make the world safer. Once submariners had demonstrated the effectiveness of undersea boats by successfully attacking some ships, possibly destroying some fleets, traditional naval warfare would cease. Another of Fulton's arguments was that if both sides in a conflict possessed deadly submarines, neither side would risk attacking the other and provoking a counterattack. The result would be peace. Long after Fulton's time, these questions and arguments about submarine warfare would be raised again and again.

In 1799 the French government agreed to sponsor the building of Fulton's submarine. The *Nautilus* was a 21-foot (6.4-meter) cylinder of copper sheets over an iron framework, with a hollow iron tube serving as a ballast tank. Like Bushnell's *Turtle,* it was driven by a hand-cranked propeller when underwater. Unlike the *Turtle,* though, the *Nautilus* had a sail on top so that when it was on the surface it could be powered by the wind. It held a three-person crew: one to turn the propeller, one to steer, and one to operate the valves and pumps of the ballast tube to control the

boat's depth. The *Nautilus* towed a single mine at the end of a line; the idea was that the sub would sneak up on an enemy ship and make a sharp turn, snapping the mine into the ship's hull.

The *Nautilus* featured several important design elements. It had diving planes, a pair of fins that guided the boat downward. This meant that the *Nautilus* could be steered as it descended. Fulton also attached a periscope to the top of the submarine. This was a tube with lenses and mirrors at each end. When it was held upright, someone looking into the bottom end could see whatever was within the field of view of the top end. Periscopes had been in use on land for several hundred years; people sometimes employed them to see over the heads of crowds.

American Robert Fulton's submarine performed successfully, but when the French, British, and American governments refused to buy it, the inventor turned his attention to steamboats. French author Jules Verne later borrowed the name of Fulton's sub, *Nautilus,* for the undersea boat in his novel *Twenty Thousand Leagues Under the Sea.*

By placing a periscope on the *Nautilus,* Fulton gave his submarine eyes. When the boat was near the surface but not above it, the periscope extended out of the water to give the pilot below a view of the action above. Along with diving planes, the periscope would become standard equipment on modern submarines.

Fulton tested the *Nautilus* successfully several times in the Seine River and the English Channel. In the end, though, despite the submarine's good performance in tests, the French government refused to use it. The limits of human-powered propulsion meant that the *Nautilus* was too slow and had too short a range to be useful on a large scale. Many observers—including the powerful Napoléon Bonaparte—doubted that it would work well in actual combat. Furthermore, some members of the government did not want France to employ a morally dubious new weapon. A minister of the navy, for example, considered the submarine fit only for pirates.

Fulton's next move suggested to some critics that he was more interested in profit than in helping France. The inventor secretly traveled to England and offered to sell his submarine plans to the British navy. Prime Minister William Pitt was interested, but he wanted Fulton to work first on other ways of destroying ships with underwater mines (also called torpedoes at that time). Fulton consented, designing a simple wooden raft that floated just below the surface of the water. Paddled by a sailor wearing dark clothing, it was almost invisible at night. The raft towed a mine with a timer. When the sailor reached an enemy ship, he would fasten the mine to it and paddle away. Fulton successfully demonstrated this technique, but the British public reacted with outrage, calling the method of attack "cowardly." At the time, the government official in charge of Great Britain's navy was the Earl of St. Vincent. Firmly opposed to both the underwater mine and the submarine, St. Vincent reportedly called Pitt "the greatest fool that ever existed to encourage a mode of war which those who command the sea do not want and which, if successful, will deprive them of it."

With no hope of sponsorship from a European government, Fulton dismantled the *Nautilus* and sold it as scrap. He returned to the United States in 1806 and discovered that the U.S. government was not interested in his submarine, either. Soon, however, Fulton and a business partner became involved in the enterprise for which Fulton is most often remembered: developing the first commercially successful steamboat.

The potential advantages that submarines offered in wartime had been known ever since John Wilkins's *Mathematicall Magick,* but the world's navies hesitated to embrace the notion of underwater craft. The early subs worked inconsistently, when they worked at all. A well-funded research program supported by a navy or government would probably have led to a dependable model, but instead development remained in the hands of a few independent inventors, most of them short of funds. Some drew on the innovations and breakthroughs of earlier inventors, while others worked in isolation. One of these lonely pioneers was an Indiana shoemaker named Lodner D. Phillips. In the mid-nineteenth century Philips built a submarine that, he claimed, could reach depths of 100 feet (30 meters). He offered it to the U.S. Navy but was told that "the boats used by the Navy go on not under the water." Nothing more was heard from Phillips.

The development of the submarine fell to others. One key figure was Wilhelm Bauer of Germany, who in 1850 built a 26.5-foot (8-meter) copper-clad boat called the *Brandtaucher* (Fire Diver). Bauer came up with an ingenious solution to the problem of maintaining trim, or balance. His sub was fitted with a weight that moved back and forth on a track. By shifting the weight, Bauer could keep the boat level. On its second sea trial, the "Diver" lived up to its name—too much so. After springing a leak, it plunged nose-first to the bottom, 60 feet (18.3 meters) down. At this unforeseen turn of events, Bauer earned his place in submarine history. Knowing that it would be impossible to open the submarine's hatch against the pressure of the outside water, he kept his two crewmen calm as water seeped into the boat. After six hours, enough water had entered that the pressure of the water on the inside walls of the submarine was almost the same as that on the outside walls, which meant that the

WILHELM BAUER OF GERMANY BUILT SEVERAL HUMAN-POWERED SUBMARINES IN THE MID-NINETEENTH CENTURY. HE ALSO LED THE FIRST RECORDED ESCAPE FROM A SUNKEN SUBMARINE.

hatch would open outward. Bauer and his men were able to take a deep breath of the remaining air, open the hatch, and swim to the surface. They made the first submarine escape.

The *Brandtaucher* had been driven by two men moving on a treadmill connected to the propeller. Recognizing the limits of human propulsion, Bauer experimented with various engine designs, but without success. He also peddled his plan to various European governments, and in 1855 Russia showed interest. Bauer went to Saint Petersburg and built a 52-foot (15.8-meter) submarine called the *Seeteufel* (Sea Devil). Powered by a four-man treadmill, the *Seeteufel* carried a 500-pound (227-kilogram) bomb. The Grand Duke Constantine, who had paid for the submarine's construction, called it "the single most devastating naval weapon known to man." The *Seeteufel*'s most impressive performance, though, was at the anniversary of the coronation of Tsar Alexander II. Bauer took four musicians beneath the surface of the harbor, and

nearby crowds heard the Russian national anthem coming from beneath the waves. A short time later, during another demonstration, the submarine ran aground and had to be abandoned. The devastating weapon was never used in war.

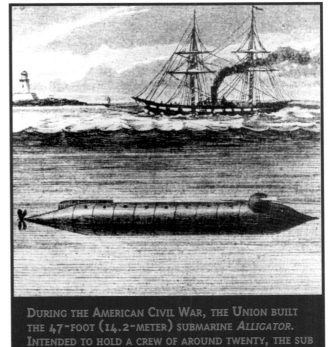

DURING THE AMERICAN CIVIL WAR, THE UNION BUILT THE 47-FOOT (14.2-METER) SUBMARINE *ALLIGATOR*. INTENDED TO HOLD A CREW OF AROUND TWENTY, THE SUB SANK BEFORE BEING USED.

Less than a decade later, during the American Civil War, naval history was made when, for the first time, a submarine sank a warship. Both sides in the conflict used submarines—or tried to. The North, or Union, tried first with the *Alligator,* a human-powered submarine designed in France. Its most important innovation was a diver's lock, a sealable hatchway that would let someone leave the boat while it was underwater in order to plant mines on enemy ships. The *Alligator* was 45 feet (14 meters) long, with a crew of twenty. In 1863, while being towed to its first combat mission in Charleston, South Carolina, it was lost in a storm at sea. A team of marine explorers began searching the area in 2004, hoping to recover the wreck of the *Alligator*, but so far it has not turned up.

The South, or Confederacy, suffered greatly from naval blockades that kept supplies from reaching its ports. Confederate leaders offered a bounty for each Union ship sunk. So one Southern company built submersible war craft as a business venture, with the idea of collecting bounties. Designed by a Confederate army officer named Francis D. Lee, these craft were not true submarines but semi-submersible, low-riding miniature steamships called Davids, after the biblical story of the warrior David who brought down a giant. They traveled awash, just barely breaking the surface, with an open hatch so that air—necessary for steam engines to operate—could freely enter. A spar or pole stuck out in front, holding a torpedo. At least nine of these vessels were manufactured, but as historian Edward Horton wrote in *The Illustrated History of the Submarine* (1974), the David "has a strong claim to being the most hazardous warship ever conceived." In addition to the risk of being blown up if the torpedo struck anything, a David could fill with water and sink if it lost a little buoyancy or if sudden waves overtopped its open hatch. No one knows how many Davids went into action, but they scored only one victory, and that was a small one. In October 1863, a David attacked the Union ironclad warship *New Ironsides* outside Charleston harbor. The resulting explosion damaged the *New Ironsides* only slightly, and the David sank while making its escape, although some of its crew survived.

The Confederacy also experimented with true submarines. The effort was spearheaded by a cotton dealer named Horace L. Hunley, who formed a company to finance and build undersea boats. The group's first effort, the *Pioneer*, was successfully tested in Lake Ponchartrain, Louisiana, but before it could be put to use, Union forces captured New Orleans and seized the

THE *H. L. HUNLEY*, NAMED FOR A SOUTHERN COTTON DEALER WHO FINANCED ITS BUILDING AND PERISHED WHILE TESTING IT, WAS ONE OF SEVERAL CONFEDERATE SUBMARINES. AFTER SINKING AN ENEMY WARSHIP, THE *HUNLEY* ITSELF SANK. DIVERS LOCATED THE WRECK IN 1995, WITH SKELETONS OF EIGHT CREWMEN STILL SITTING AT THE CRANKSHAFT THEY HAD TURNED TO PROPEL THE BOAT.

sub, which was later sold for scrap. Hunley's second effort, the *American Diver,* never saw combat and sank while being towed. The company's third boat met a more dramatic fate. This submarine was a converted steam boiler. About 40 feet (12.2 meters) long, driven by eight men turning a crankshaft attached to a rear propeller, it had diving planes, ballast tanks, and two manholes made of thick glass in the upper deck. Like the Davids, it was armed with a bomb mounted on a harpoon.

This submarine's weaknesses soon became tragically evident. On its first trial, the boat lost trim suddenly and plunged downward. Because the crew had left the manholes open, for easier breathing or because the 4-foot-wide (1.2-meter-wide) submarine was dark and uncomfortable with them closed, the boat sank at once, with the loss of five men. On its next trial, its became stuck in the muddy seabed and flooded. Its entire crew, including Hunley, perished. The company raised and repaired the unfortunate submarine and named it the *H. L. Hunley,* although by then it had also acquired the nickname Peripatetic—meaning "traveling"—Coffin. Volunteers stepped forward to try again, and on the night of February 17, 1864, the *Hunley* moved silently toward the USS *Housatonic,* one of the ships blockading Charleston. As the submarine approached the ship at a depth of about 2 feet (0.6 meters), crewmen aboard the *Housatonic* spotted it and opened fire. The *Hunley*'s crew fired their bomb-carrying harpoon, and the charge tore a huge hole in the hull of the *Housatonic,* which sank within minutes. This historic success came at a high price, though. Neither the *Hunley* nor any of her crew returned from the mission. In 1995 divers located the wreck of the *Hunley,* which they later raised for study and preservation. Experts now think that the submarine probably sank when a Union boat, hurrying to the aid of the *Housatonic* survivors, swamped the sub's open hatch with its wake.

The Civil War produced one other submarine: a 28-foot (8.5-meter) boat that its owner, American Oliver Halstead, called the *Intelligent Whale.* It was to be powered by a propeller hand-turned by as many as thirteen crewmen. Halstead began building the submarine during the war, funded by Union investors who hoped, like the Southern company

THE *INTELLIGENT WHALE* WAS THE LAST OF THE CIVIL WAR—ERA SUBMARINES. THE U.S. NAVY BOUGHT THE SUB BUT FOUND IT DANGEROUS AND UNUSABLE. THE *WHALE* IS SAID TO HAVE DROWNED SEVERAL DOZEN MEN BEFORE THE NAVY GAVE UP ON IT.

that produced the Davids, to make money on bounties. After President Abraham Lincoln refused to approve private military operations, the investors abandoned the project. Halstead finished building the *Whale* in 1866 and later sold it to the U.S. Navy, but the craft flooded on its first test and was never used.

Unlike many early submarines, the *Intelligent Whale* escaped the scrapyard. It rests in the National Guard Militia Museum of New Jersey, a monument to the high hopes of inventors who dreamed of traveling under the sea using human power. The next stage in submarine development would harness mechanical power sources. The result would be a truly useful underwater boat.

THE LARGE FRENCH BOAT *Le Plongeur* WAS THE FIRST SUBMARINE WITH AN ENGINE. A FEATURE THAT BECAME STANDARD ON LATER SUBS WAS ITS CONNING TOWER, THE TURRETLIKE STRUCTURE ON THE UPPER DECK. THE CONNING TOWER CONTAINED A HATCH FOR ENTERING THE SUB AND SERVED AS A COMMAND POST WHEN THE SUB WAS ON THE SURFACE.

THREE

The Submarine Comes of Age

The *Hunley* showed that a submarine could sink a ship. A few years later, in 1866, an English engineer named Robert Whitehead created the perfect submarine weapon: the first self-propelled mine, which he called a torpedo. Unlike earlier mines and torpedoes, which either floated into enemy ships or were shot or attached from up close, Whitehead torpedoes were fired from a distance. Compressed air propelled them toward their targets. Although the world's navies immediately adopted this innovation for use by surface boats, the new weapon also made submarine warfare possible. But the *Hunley* and every other early submarine had also shown that human-powered undersea craft were slow, limited in range, and dangerously unreliable. Even before the *Hunley*'s heroic mission, European inventors were looking for other ways to power submarines.

The French navy launched the world's first mechanical submarine in 1863. Compressed air powered an 80-horsepower engine that drove the 140-foot (42.7-meter) boat, called *Le Plongeur* (The Diver). The sub was huge by the standards of its time. It had to be, to hold the necessary supply of compressed-air tanks. The engine worked, but *Le Plongeur* had other problems. The biggest challenge concerned the depth line, an imaginary line through the length of the submarine from which the boat's depth below the surface is measured. *Le Plongeur* suffered from what submarine designers call longitudinal instability—that is, difficulty keeping its depth line stable. The sub showed a disturbing tendency to plummet downward out of control. When its operators tried to correct course and stabilize the depth line, the sub would lunge upward with equal wildness. *Le Plongeur,* the first submarine to travel by means other than muscle power, was never used.

In 1864 Wilhelm Bauer, inventor of the ill-fated *Brandtaucher* and *Seeteufel,* suggested that a submarine could be driven by an internal-combustion engine, based on the same principle as the engines that power modern automobiles. A different idea appeared six years later, in French author Jules Verne's novel *Twenty Thousand Leagues under the Sea.* This enormously popular book introduced a famous fictional submarine: the *Nautilus,* commanded by a renegade named Nemo. When one of the book's characters asks Nemo about the *Nautilus*'s power source, Nemo boasts that the sub runs on electricity—a new and exciting scientific frontier in Verne's time. Nemo's explanation of how the submarine gets the electricity is quite vague, but scholars think that Verne envisioned using chemicals from seawater, or undersea minerals, in some sort of battery.

Neither the internal-combustion engine nor the electrical battery was yet practical for submarine use, so inventors turned to the power that had revolutionized industry, railroads, and shipping in the nineteenth century: steam. By the 1870s, British engineers had produced steam engines that were small and efficient enough to be used in submarines. Steam brought its own set of problems, however. A steam engine is basically a fire that heats water in a boiler, producing steam that drives machinery. But fire requires oxygen. At the surface, a submarine could travel under steam power, with its hatchway open to admit air. Before it could submerge, however, the fire had to be shut down or it would use up all the sub's oxygen. The new steam engines could be temporarily sealed, leaving a reservoir of heat that would continue to produce steam for a few hours, but the stored heat would make a closed

AN ENGLISH CLERGYMAN BUILT THE FIRST STEAM-POWERED SUBMARINE, THE *RESURGAM*. THE SUB'S NAME MEANS "I WILL RISE," BUT THE BOAT SANK AT SEA SOON AFTER IT WAS COMPLETED. IN 1995 A FISHING VESSEL'S NETS SNAGGED ON SOMETHING THAT PROVED TO BE THE WRECK OF THIS EARLY SUBMARINE.

submarine hideously uncomfortable. In addition, because the process of sealing the engine took at least twenty minutes, a steam-powered sub could not dive quickly—and delay would be a grave handicap in combat.

The first to build a steam sub was an English clergyman named George Garrett. Although he claimed to be interested primarily in undersea exploration, his 45-foot (13.7-meter) boat, the *Resurgam* (Latin for "I will rise"), was equipped with two Whitehead torpedoes. The Admiralty, the British naval bureau, was still skeptical about submarines, but in 1879 officials agreed to observe sea trials of the *Resurgam*. The submarine traveled partway to the trial site under its own steam, but high temperatures from the boiler and other problems caused Garrett to request a tow for the rest of the trip. While the *Resurgam* was being towed, it flooded and sank, but Garrett's career in submarines did not sink with her. He later joined forces with Thorsten Nordenfeldt, a Swedish manufacturer of machine guns, to design and produce a series of submarines called the Nordenfeldt boats. By this time, navies around the world were becoming increasingly interested in the possibilities of submarine power. Nordenfeldt, a successful businessman and salesman, made sure that his new product received a lot of attention by inviting members of Europe's royal families to witness a series of sea trials. The resulting publicity, combined with Nordenfeldt's reputation, helped him sell submarines to the Greek, Turkish, and Russian navies. None of these boats proved usable. Like *Le Plongeur,* they could not maintain a level depth line. Describing the submarine Nordenfeldt sold to Turkey, one engineer wrote, "Nothing could be imagined more unstable than this Turkish boat. . . . She was perpetually working up and

SUBMARINES RECEIVED MUCH PUBLICITY IN THE LATE NINETEENTH CENTURY THROUGH THE EFFORTS OF THORSTEN NORDENFELDT, A SWEDISH INDUSTRIALIST. NORDENFELDT PRODUCED A HANDFUL OF STEAM-POWERED SUBMARINES LIKE THIS ONE AND SOLD THEM, WITH GREAT

down . . . and no human vigilance could keep her on an even keel for half a minute at a time."

As Garrett and Nordenfeldt had discovered, a steam submarine was almost impossible to keep level. Its boiler always contained water, which constantly sloshed back and forth, causing the submarine to tilt uncontrollably. For submarines to become workable and practical, they needed a different power source. Battery technology was rapidly improving, and during the 1880s French designers produced a series of submarines driven by battery-powered electric motors. One of them, the 59-foot (18-meter) *Gymnôte,* launched in 1888, used 204 batteries and featured an important innovation—a pump that used compressed

FANFARE, TO VARIOUS NAVIES. ALTHOUGH NONE OF HIS BOATS WAS SUCCESSFUL, NORDENFELDT FUELED INTEREST IN SUBMARINES AMONG BOTH GOVERNMENTS AND THE GENERAL PUBLIC.

air to force water quickly out of the ballast tank, improving the operator's control of the boat. The *Gymnôte* made more than two hundred successful dives and was accepted by the French navy, which then authorized its builder, Gustave Zédé, to produce a bigger submarine. He built the modestly named 159-foot (48.5-meter) *Gustave Zédé* out of bronze and equipped it with the first internal torpedo tube. The boat's great length made it unstable and difficult to operate, while fumes given off by its batteries made it extremely uncomfortable. Despite many attempts to correct its flaws, the *Gustave Zédé* was never a success.

The French government had become seriously interested in developing a working submarine fleet. In 1898 the navy announced a contest for boat designers, who were invited to submit plans for a particular

THE SELF-PROPELLED TORPEDO, INVENTED IN THE LATE NINETEENTH CENTURY, WAS FIRST USED BY SURFACE VESSELS. BEFORE LONG, HOWEVER, SUBMARINE DESIGNERS ADDED THE NEW WEAPON INTO THEIR PLANS FOR UNDERSEA CRAFT. NOTE THE TWO TORPEDOES STOWED UNDER THE CONTROL ROOM OF THIS SUB, AND THE LAUNCH TUBE OPENING OUT OF THE BOW.

kind of craft—not so much a true submarine as a torpedo boat that could submerge for short periods. It had to be able to reach high speeds on the surface, where it would travel most of the time. Once near its target, it would submerge, approach the enemy ship unseen, and fire its torpedoes. The winner was Maxime Laubeuf, and the French navy built his boat, the *Narval.* It was the first double-hulled submarine, with an outer hull shaped like that of a surface boat, for greater speed and maneuverability on the surface, and an inner hull designed to withstand the water pressure below. The space between the two hulls held the ballast tanks. The *Narval's* most important innovation was its power system. It had a steam engine that not only powered the boat at the surface but also produced energy to charge the batteries that drove the boat when it submerged. This made the *Narval* the first submarine with rechargeable batteries. In theory, it could remain at sea for a long time without having to refuel. The French navy immediately started building more boats modeled on the *Narval,* making France, at the dawn of the twentieth century, the world leader in submarine technology.

Spanish and Polish inventors also produced working submarines during this period. In 1890 Spanish designer Isaac Peral's unnamed sub became the first to launch a torpedo underwater. Despite Peral's success, the Spanish government was focused on other things and decided not to develop a submarine program. Peral's invention, however, was preserved and is now on display in Cartagena, Spain.

In the wake of these advances and successful tests, the American government began to change its attitude toward submarines. Soon the United States was trying to catch up to France. In 1893 the navy declared that it would purchase the best design for a military submarine. The winner of the competition was John P. Holland, a former schoolteacher in New Jersey, who had been trying to sell his submarine plans to the government for almost twenty years. More than any other individual, Holland turned the temperamental, hard-to-control submarine into a practical modern craft, though his road to success was long and rocky.

Born in Ireland, Holland came to the United States in 1873. Like Robert

Fulton several generations earlier, he resented British power and was inter-ested in submarines partly because he believed they would be the perfect weapon against the British navy. In 1875 he tried to sell a submarine plan to the U.S. Navy, which wasn't interested—perhaps because just a few years earlier the navy had paid $50,000 for the *Intelligent Whale*, an embarassing failure. Soon, though, Holland found financial backing from the Fenian So-ciety, a group of Irish Americans willing to use guerrilla or terrorist tactics against Great Britain. The Fenians wanted Holland to build an underwater gunboat for them to use in British ports. In doing so, Holland made his first historic contribution to submarine design by using a tiny 4-horsepower gasoline engine as a power source. For the first time, the recently developed internal-combustion engine had been used in a submarine. Although the boat, now known as *Holland I*, was small, slow, and almost useless, it im-pressed the Fenians, who funded the building of a bigger, faster sub. This was the 31-foot (9.4-meter), three-man *Holland II*, better known as the *Fenian Ram*. Launched in 1881, it was powered by a 15-horsepower engine. When the submarine was below the surface, the engine fumes were vented through a valve, while bottles of compressed air supplied the crew with oxygen. The sub was armed with a gun that used compressed air to fire an explosive projectile.

The *Fenian Ram*'s most important features were Holland's revolu-tionary approaches to ballast and buoyancy. With this boat, Holland solved the problems of longitudinal instability and poor control that had dogged earlier submarine pioneers. To sink below the surface, a boat needs ballast. By Holland's time, all submarines used water as ballast. With an endless supply close at hand, submariners can easily add or re-move it at will. But ballast tanks, like steam boilers, posed a problem. Whenever they were partly full, which was most of the time, the water sloshed around in them, altering the boat's trim. Holland's solution was to keep large ballast tanks completely full at all times and use a series of small tanks to adjust buoyancy. These tanks' free surfaces—the term submarine designers use for the surface area of "sloshable" water—would be small enough not to cause erratic handling or lurching instability. Holland eventually received patents for the clever systems of piping he invented to control the flow of ballast.

As for buoyancy, all earlier submarines had been ballasted to zero buoyancy in order to submerge. In other words, they were made as heavy as possible, with ballast tanks full, and simply sank straight down. When their ballast was emptied, they rose straight up again. Holland wanted a submarine that could be steered while it was submerging and surfacing—a submarine that could be driven down at an angle rather than passively submitting to gravity and sinking with a level keel. To achieve this goal, Holland drew on Fulton's earlier development, the diving plane, and on his own studies of how air and water moving over wings create the driving force known as lift. The result was a set of movable diving rudders or planes, set horizontally along the rear of the submarine, that were much more responsive to controls than Fulton's earlier design. Holland always kept a reserve of positive buoyancy. He accomplished this in two ways: by not filling his small ballast tanks completely and by maintaining reservoirs of compressed air. This slight positive buoyancy meant that the sub would not sink, but it could be driven down into the water by the downward angle of the diving planes as the engine pushed it forward. In a way, the *Fenian Ram* looked back not just to Fulton's diving planes but also to the first submarine, Cornelis Drebbel's rowboat with the slanted forward deck, which also submerged when propelled forward. By combining the concept of the diving plane with the power of the internal-combustion engine and his innovations in ballasting, Holland produced a submarine that acted almost like a boat that could fly underwater. Some marine historians consider the *Fenian Ram* the first truly modern submarine.

The *Fenian Ram* proved very successful, but Holland wasn't fully satisfied with it. For two and a half years he puttered up and down the Hudson River between New Jersey and Manhattan, testing his submarine, ironing out its problems, and fine-tuning its performance. His was the spirit of a true inventor—but his backers, the Fenians, had a mission in mind. They grew so impatient with Holland's prolonged trial period that in late 1883 they simply stole the submarine and towed it away. The Fenians found themselves unable to use the *Ram,* though, so they abandoned it. Holland could not reclaim it—after all, the Fenians had paid for it. He simply turned his back on the submarine and the Fenians altogether. Eventually the *Fenian Ram* wound up in a museum in Paterson, New Jersey, along with its predecessor, *Holland I.*

Holland had often criticized the U.S. military for its lack of interest in his submarines. In a newspaper article titled "Can New York Be Bombarded?," he tried to alarm the public about the possibility of a submarine attack on an American city. He had also complained that "the navy doesn't like submarines because there's no deck to strut on." In 1888, however, the navy indicated its changing opinion of submarines by announcing a design competition. Thorsten Nordenfeldt entered the competition, as did a San Francisco–based submarine designer named J.H.L. Tuck, who had pioneered a steam engine powered by powdered caustic soda rather than oil or coal. The navy liked Holland's proposal best, but even Holland had failed to meet all of the requirements set forth in the competition rules, so the government took no immediate action. Five years later, the navy announced a second competition. Although the standards it set were unrealistic and contrary to Holland's design style, Holland again submitted a proposal. This time his main competitor was Simon Lake, who had designed the *Argonaut,* a 36-foot (11-meter) submarine that could roll along the sea bottom on wheels. The *Argonaut* was meant for salvage operations in shallow water—in fact, Lake and a friend had spent many hours in an earlier version of it, happily gathering oysters and clams from the floor of New York Bay. Lake pointed out to the navy that his boat would be useful for clearing underwater mines, or for laying them. Holland's proposal, however, came closer to meeting the navy's requirements and was named the winner. Two years later Holland received the $150,000 award and began building the *Plunger,* as the craft was called.

From the start, Holland knew that the *Plunger* was a bad idea. The navy wanted more speed than a gasoline engine could provide, so the *Plunger* had a steam engine. At the same time, the navy wanted a submarine that

HOLLAND'S CHIEF RIVAL IN SUBMARINE DESIGN WAS SIMON LAKE, WHOSE *ARGONAUT* HAD WHEELS FOR ROLLING ACROSS THE SEAFLOOR. ALTHOUGH LAKE'S SUB COULD PERFORM TASKS SUCH AS MOVING THROUGH A HARBOR MINEFIELD SAFELY BELOW THE LEVEL OF THE EXPLOSIVE DEVICES, AS SHOWN HERE, DRIVING ON THE OCEAN BOTTOM WAS IMPRACTICAL, AND THE DESIGN NEVER BECAME POPULAR.

could submerge in one minute, which was impossible with steam. The steam-heat problem also remained—during one trial, running at two-thirds power, the temperature in the boiler room reached 137 degrees Fahrenheit (59 degrees Celsius). In addition, the navy insisted that the boat submerge with a level keel, which was exactly the opposite of Holland's new approach to submarining. Realizing that the navy's requirements could not be met, Holland stopped working on the *Plunger* and returned the money. At the same time, he scraped up enough private financial backing to build a submarine on his own—the kind of submarine he knew should be built. He planned to show it to the navy when it was completed.

The result was the *Holland VI*, launched in 1897. Marine historians who do not identify the *Fenian Ram* as the first truly modern submarine usually give that title to the 54-foot (16.5-meter) *Holland VI*. Powered by a 50-horsepower gasoline engine that could either drive the propeller directly or charge electrical batteries, the *Holland VI* could carry enough gasoline to let it travel about 1,000 miles (1,609 kilometers) without refueling. The submarine held a crew of six and displayed the results of Holland's long and painstaking work on the control of ballast, trim, stability, and diving planes. It could also fire Whitehead torpedoes. Was the navy, Holland asked, interested in buying it? While the navy considered the offer, Holland kept refining and tinkering with the submarine. He eventually ran out of money and lost control of his private company to another firm, the Electric Boat Company.

The government did buy the *Holland VI* at last. In 1900 it was commissioned as the USS *Holland* (later known as the *SS-1*), the first submarine in the U.S. Navy. Orders poured in to the Electric Boat Company. The U.S. Navy wanted more "Holland boats." The British, Dutch, and Japanese governments placed orders, too.

Once the Holland boat had made the submarine a practical proposition, the early years of the twentieth century saw a gradual buildup of submarine forces around the world. For a while, France stayed at the forefront. Following Holland's lead, French designers experimented with gasoline-fueled internal-combustion engines, but France also built more steam-powered submarines like the *Narval.* Because steam-powered submarines were still faster than those powered by internal combustion, some designers continued to try to solve the problems connected with the use of steam engines on submarines. Others tackled the gasoline engine's problems, chiefly the danger posed by toxic, explosive fumes.

Simon Lake, the oyster-gathering designer of the wheeled *Argonaut,* took advantage of the

IN 1900 JOHN P. HOLLAND'S SIXTH SUBMARINE BECAME THE USS *HOLLAND,* THE FIRST UNDERWATER BOAT COMMISSIONED INTO THE U.S. NAVY. THE "HOLLAND BOAT," AS IT WAS CALLED, WAS THE FOUNDATION OF THE AMERICAN AND BRITISH SUBMARINE FLEET.

submarine boom. He invented many submarine innovations, including a collapsible periscope, and he formed a company that sold gasoline-powered boats to Russia, Germany, and Austria. A few years later, Lake also designed several submarines for the United States, including one that set a new depth-diving record of 256 feet (78 meters) in 1912. Submarine development in the U.S. Navy, however, focused mainly on enlarging and improving the Holland submarine.

By this time Holland himself was out of the picture. Despite the success of the *Holland VI,* the inventor had little influence in operations and business decisions of the Electric Boat Company, which owned his patents. In 1904 Holland resigned from the company, owning just 0.5 percent of its stock. He died ten years later, less than a month before the first submarine attack of World War I—the war that would show the world what submarines could do.

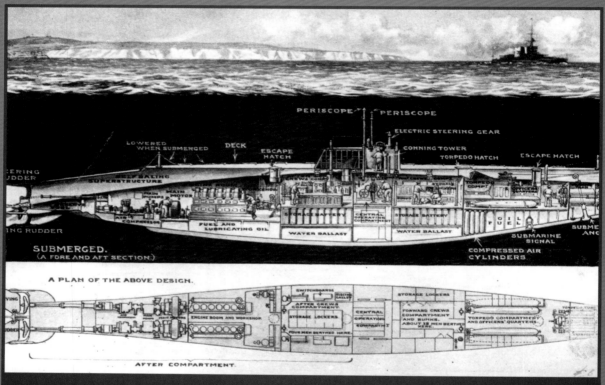

PERISCOPE   PERISCOPE

ELECTRIC STEERING GEAR

LOWERED
WHEN SUBMERGED   DECK   ESCAPE
HATCH   COMNING TOWER   TORPEDO HATCH   ESCAPE HATCH

EERING
UDDER
                    SELF-BALING
                    SUPERSTRUCTURE
                              MAIN
                              MOTOR
            AIR
            COMPRESSOR
ING RUDDER   FUEL AND
                    LUBRICATING OIL   STORAGE BATTERY   CENTRAL
OPERATING
COMPARTMENT   STORAGE BATTERY   FUEL   OIL
FUEL   SUBME
ANC

SUBMERGED.
(A FORE AND AFT SECTION.)
                    WATER BALLAST   WATER BALLAST   SUBMARINE
SIGNAL   COMPRESSED AIR
CYLINDERS

A PLAN OF THE ABOVE DESIGN.

VING   SWITCHBOARDS   ELECTRIC
GALLEY   STORAGE LOCKERS
          AFTER CREWS
          COMPARTMENT
UDDER   ENGINE ROOM AND WORKSHOP   STORAGE LOCKERS   CENTRAL
OPERATING
COMPARTMENT   FORWARD CREWS
COMPARTMENT
AND BUNKS.
ABOUT 18 MEN BERTH
HERE.   TORPEDO COMPARTMENT
AND OFFICERS' QUARTERS.   TORPEDO TUBE
          FOUR MEN BERTHED HERE.

AFTER COMPARTMENT.

WORLD WAR I (1914–1918) WAS FOUGHT BELOW THE WAVES AS WELL AS ON THEM. PUBLISHED IN GREAT
BRITAIN FIVE MONTHS AFTER THE START OF THE WAR, A DIAGRAM FROM THE *ILLUSTRATED WAR NEWS* SHOWS THE
LAYOUT OF THE BRITISH HOLLAND SUBS. THE WHITE CLIFFS OF DOVER, A LANDMARK OF THE ENGLISH COASTLINE,
APPEAR IN THE BACKGROUND, REMINDING READERS THAT SUBMARINES WERE GUARDING THEIR COASTAL WATERS.

U-Boats and the New Naval Warfare

A century after the Earl of St. Vincent scornfully
dismissed interest in submarines as foolish, Great Britain reluctantly
entered the submarine era. Many members of the royal navy still felt
that submarines were, in the words of Admiral A. K. "Tug" Wilson, "un-
derhand, unfair, and damned un-English." Yet as other nations bought
and built submarines, the British realized that they could not afford to
stay out of this new arms race much longer.

Having decided to acquire submarines, the royal navy ordered some
Holland boats, arranging with the Electric Boat Company that the subs
be built in Britain under the supervision of American engineers. This
arrangement gave British designers and boatbuilders a crash course in
submarine design and construction. Almost immediately they began
improving the Holland boat. They produced several new series of submarines, some designed for coastal patrols, others built for long-distance overseas service. Their most important technical innovation was
replacing Holland's gasoline-powered internal-combustion engine with
a new invention first perfected in Germany in 1897—the diesel engine. Unlike the internal-combustion engine, which uses a spark to ig-
nite a mixture of fuel and air, the diesel engine compresses air, raising
its temperature to the point where the compressed air ignites the fuel,

producing power that can be used to drive machinery or charge electrical batteries. The diesel engine had many advantages for use on submarines. It was more efficient, generating more power from cheaper fuel than the gasoline engine, and it was also safer. Soon diesel engines became standard for submarines, although France continued to experiment with steam power.

Britain's leaders in general remained skeptical about submarines. Many said that undersea craft were an underdog's weapon. Real sea power, they claimed, had always rested and would always rest with the mightiest surface navy. But the country's First Sea Lord for most of the period from 1904 to 1915, Admiral John A. "Jacky" Fisher, was more far sighted. In 1904 he wrote, "It is astounding to me, perfectly astounding, how the very best among us fail to realize the vast impending revolution in Naval warfare and Naval strategy that the submarine will accomplish . . . it is enough to make your hair stand on end!"

Strategy aside, living conditions on the early submarines were enough to make anyone's hair stand on end. With a bucket for a toilet and no water to spare for such luxuries as bathing, submarine duty tested the spirits of officers and crewmen alike. "The discomforts in submarines cannot be exaggerated," wrote a Royal Navy captain in 1910. He gave details:

> Clothes cannot be dried, fires are not permissible, in cold weather it is difficult to keep reasonably warm, the amount of fresh water precludes any attempt at personal cleanliness and the roar of the Engines is all over the boat. . . . To many the smell inside a submarine after she has been a short time at sea, which is absolutely peculiar to itself, is most revolting. All food tastes of it, clothes reek of it, it is quite impossible to wear any clothes again after they have been used in it.

Smelly or not, submarines had become part of the Royal Navy. The great majority of them were designed for coastal defense—Great

Britain, after all, is an island nation, with plenty of coast to defend. By 1914 Great Britain had seventy-five subs in service and was building nearly thirty more. At the time this was the largest submarine fleet in the world. It was not, however, the most formidable. That distinction went to Germany's *Unterseeboote* (undersea boats), better known as U-boats.

Like Great Britain, Germany was slow to embrace the submarine. The German navy had shown interest in Nordenfeldt boats until they were revealed to be useless failures. For years afterward, Admiral Alfred von Tirpitz, head of the navy, dismissed submarines as a waste of time—useful for coastal defense, perhaps, but not important to Germany, which had little coast to defend. Yet by 1904, with Japan and Russia buying undersea boats and Britain launching its submarine program, Germany decided that it, too, needed submarines. At this point, von Tirpitz and other leaders made a crucial decision—from the start, Germany would use submarines for attacking enemy fleets as well as defending its own ships and coastline.

A German U-boat at sea. World War I submarines traveled on the surface, submerging when necessary for concealment or to approach a target.

At first, Germany built U-boats powered by paraffin or kerosene engines. By 1910, however, the navy was taking advantage of Germany's leadership in diesel design and construction to equip its subs with the best engines then available in the world. Because Germany manufactured top-quality optical and scientific instruments, the U-boats also had excellent periscopes and navigation equipment. The German navy created an intense and highly effective training program for submarine officers and crew, and by 1914 its submarine fleet numbered twenty-eight U-boats, including ten that were 210 feet (64 meters) or more in length. These long-distance, high-speed subs were designed specifically to attack merchant ships. They would soon make naval history.

When World War I erupted in Europe in August 1914, a web of alliances drew many nations into the conflict. As far as the naval part of the war was concerned, however, the main combatants were Great Britain against Germany; the United States supported Britain with shipments of supplies but did not enter the war until 1917.

A week into the war, a British ship rammed and sank a U-boat. A month later, the *U21* fired a torpedo at the British cruiser *Pathfinder,* which sank with 250 men. The war beneath the waves had begun. Anyone who had not yet realized the threat posed by submarines learned to fear them on September 22, 1914. That day the *U9* surfaced off the Dutch coast and spotted three British cruisers steaming along. The *Hogue, Aboukir,* and *Cressy* were creaky old vessels whose commanders were not following the rules that the Royal Navy had hastily laid down for avoiding submarine fire. They were neither zigzagging nor maintaining the recommended speed. In an episode that some Germans called "three before breakfast," the *U9* picked off all three ships with its torpedoes, sending 1,459 men to the bottom in about ninety minutes. Great Britain was stunned—and even more stunned a little more than two months later, when the *U18* managed to sneak into Scapa Flow, an island harbor north of Scotland that was the home port of most of the British fleet. The submarine was spotted and rammed before it could do any damage,

STRUCK BY A U-BOAT'S TORPEDO, A ROYAL NAVY TROOP TRANSPORT SHIP SINKS, STERN UP, IN THE NORTH ATLANTIC. MEN ARE ESCAPING IN LIFEBOATS AS MORE SURVIVORS SLIDE DOWN ROPES.

but the incident showed how easily submarines could infiltrate seemingly well-defended waters.

When the war began, neither side had any real idea of what submarines could do in combat, or how best to use them. All naval experience up to that time had been limited to surface ships, so many submarine commanders handled their craft almost as though they were surface ships. Instead of prowling the seas underwater, they spent most of their time on the surface. This had several advantages. First, although the submarines of the era were capable of staying submerged for long periods of time when necessary, they moved much more slowly underwater, using battery power, than on the surface. Second, crews greatly preferred being on the surface when possible, for better ventilation and a greater feeling of safety. As a result, World War I submarine commanders tended to submerge their boats only to avoid being sighted or when approaching targets. When the moment to attack arrived, a submarine commander could either stay submerged and fire a torpedo underwater or surface to fire a deck-mounted artillery gun, quickly resubmerging afterward. Because the supply of torpedos was always limited, commanders attacked from the surface when they could.

Submarines had three strategic roles during the conflict: reconnaissance (gathering information about enemy ship movement), warfare, and blockade. Throughout the war, submariners on both sides contributed to reconnaissance and performed heroically in many naval battles. The most outstanding battle performance was probably that of Britain's submarine force in the Dardanelles, a narrow waterway through Turkey that is part of the passage between the Aegean Sea and the Black Sea, separating Europe and Asia. This area was the scene of a major conflict between Britain and its allies and Turkey, a German ally. Braving mines, nets, patrol boats, and treacherous currents, British subs made their way through the Dardanelles to destroy numerous Turkish and German ships. One British sub alone, the *E11,* sank 122 Turkish vessels. Its commander, Martin Nasmith, made submarine history not only for this remarkably successful campaign but for his invention of periscope photography. Nasmith got his sub into Constantinople harbor, the heart of enemy shipping, and torpedoed a ship there. To prove that he had penetrated the harbor, he put a camera on top of his submarine's periscope and took a picture of a famous mosque.

Despite the Dardanelles campaign and other campaigns involving submarines in the Mediterranean, Baltic, and North seas, the sub never really tilted the overall balance of most battles. Throughout the war, Britain and its allies lost a total of thirty-nine large warships to submarine attack—not enough to interfere greatly with surface warfare. The submarine's biggest impact on the war was through blockading, especially Germany's relentless efforts to prevent merchant shipping from reaching British ports. The submarine blockade was an entirely new form of warfare, and a controversial one.

Until World War I, naval warfare had followed certain rules. The enemy's merchant ships were supposed to be attacked or arrested only if they were carrying war materials, such as weapons, which could be seized as contraband (prohibited cargo). Another class of cargo, called conditional contraband, consisted of materials that could potentially be aids to making war, such as fuel, money, and food. Conditional contraband was to be seized only if it was bound for enemy ports, not neutral ports. If a warship did attack or sink an enemy's commercial ship, it was supposed to take survivors on board, not leave them on the open water. Ships of neutral powers—nations not at war—could not be attacked, only arrested, and only if they were carrying contraband. Still another rule prohibited the laying of explosive mines in shipping lanes or waters used by neutral vessels.

These practices reflected the conditions of naval warfare before the introduction of the submarine. Submarines, it was clear, could not follow them. A submarine could not arrest a neutral ship; it would not have the extra crew to man the ship. Nor did it have the room to take on prisoners. Many people assumed that submarines simply would not attack merchant fleets and commercial ships. Early in the war, however, the question of blockades and supply lines caused both sides to bend, then break, the rules.

Germany's wartime economy depended on shipments of food and other conditional contraband imported through the Netherlands, a neutral country. Yet Great Britain, the only major seafaring country that had refused to sign an international agreement governing maritime warfare and shipping, blockaded first the English Channel and then the entire North Sea. British ships laid mines everywhere except along certain well-guarded shipping routes, and Britain warned the world that any ship that ventured outside those routes did so at its own risk. Yet British cruisers patrolled the safe routes, inspecting merchant ships. To keep supplies out of German hands, Britain was seizing conditional contraband bound for neutral ports. The British had broken international

THE GERMAN *U20* FIRED A SINGLE TORPEDO AT THE HUGE PASSENGER LINER *LUSITANIA*, WHICH SANK IN JUST TWENTY MINUTES ON MAY 7, 1915. THE TORPEDO PENETRATED THE HULL, AND A SECOND EXPLOSION TORE A HUGE HOLE BELOW THE WATERLINE. GERMANY TRIED TO ARGUE THAT THE SECOND EXPLOSION PROVED THAT THE *LUSITANIA* WAS SECRETLY AND ILLEGALLY CARRYING MUNITIONS TO GREAT BRITAIN. MODERN HISTORIANS, HOWEVER, AGREE THAT THE TORPEDO IGNITED AN EXPLOSION OF FLAMMABLE COAL DUST IN THE SHIP'S FUEL COMPARTMENTS.

maritime law, the German navy argued. Germany could not be blamed for breaking another maritime law to fight back.

In early 1915 Germany announced a blockade of its own. In the waters around Great Britain, its U-boats would attack British commercial craft on sight; Germany could not guarantee that neutral shipping would be safe, either. This policy led to one of the most scandalous incidents of the war. On May 7, 1915, off the coast of Ireland, a U-boat attacked a British passenger liner without warning. The *Lusitania* sank with the loss of around 1,200 passengers, including 128 Americans. Britain and her allies were outraged, as were the U.S. government and the American public. Sinking a passenger ship without notice seemed a far more heinous atrocity than Britain's use of mines and cargo inspections. Although Germany later attacked several more passenger ships, the navy ordered its submarine commanders to focus on warships and merchantmen—partly so that the United States would not be provoked into entering the war.

Germany's U-boat blockade of Great Britain continued throughout the four years of the war, with dramatic results in the North Sea, the waters around Great Britain, the Mediterranean Sea, and the North Atlantic Ocean. By the end of 1916, not quite two and a half years into the war, U-boats had sunk more than 2.3 million tons (2 million metric tons) of British, Allied, and neutral merchant shipping. In 1917 they sank merchant ships totalling more than 6 million tons (5.4 million metric tons). That year the United States entered the war—after British codebreakers deciphered a secret message from Germany to Mexico, in which Germany offered to give some of the United States to Mexico if Mexico entered the war and helped Germany win.

By that time, the U-boat toll on British shipping was formidable. In April 1917 alone, more than 350 merchant ships were lost—one of every four that went to sea. It was, writes military historian Edward Horton in *The Illustrated History of the Submarine,* "one of the darkest moments in British history." Yet it was not quite enough to bring Britain to its knees, as the German naval command had expected. Britain's war machine did not buckle. Meanwhile, Germany was suffering. The British blockade caused desperate shortages of food, fuel, and other essential supplies in Germany, although factories there kept turning out U-boats as fast as they could. Some of their large new long-range U-boats even ventured across the Atlantic to the east coast of the United States, although they did not attack American ships there. But in May 1917 it suddenly became much harder for U-boat commanders to sink merchant ships. Great Britain had finally adopted the convoy system.

Since ancient times, commercial and military fleets have used this "safety in numbers" method, banding together to travel as a group through enemy-infested waters. Some British leaders had objected loudly to the idea of convoys, claiming that they would give the U-boats too large and easy a target. In reality, while a cluster of thirty ships together is a tempting target, it is not that much easier to find than a single ship. When thirty targets are spread out separately, however, the chances that one or more will eventually be located and attacked are

AFTER THE UNITED STATES ENTERED THE WAR IN APRIL 1917, AMERICAN SUBMARINES AND THEIR CREWS SET OUT FROM PORT TO JOIN THE NORTH ATLANTIC CONVOYS.

greatly increased. In addition, although the Royal Navy could not provide military escorts for every single merchant ship, it could provide armed escorts for the convoys—which meant that U-boats risked being attacked in return. The United States contributed to convoy escort and patrol duties in the North Atlantic with surface ships and with its L-class submarines, the first American long-range oceangoing subs, built between 1914 and 1917. As soon as the convoy system went into effect, losses began to fall. In 1918 Britain lost less than half as much merchant tonnage as in 1917. The Allies also destroyed sixty-three U-boats in 1917 and sixty-nine in 1918.

The convoy was the most successful anti-sub tactic of the war. Earlier, Britain had experimented with other tactical measures to deceive, avoid, or locate U-boats. In addition to coastal patrol warships, the Royal Navy launched Q-ships, which were merchant ships with concealed guns on their decks (ordinary merchant vessels were unarmed). A U-boat that approached a Q-ship expecting the typical easy prey could be attacked itself by the hidden gunners. This method was not particularly successful, however. Britain lost twenty-four Q-ships to destroy seventeen U-boats. Even less successful were some more imaginative—or desperate—measures. The Royal Navy tried to train seagulls to perch on periscopes so that they could "scout" for submarines. It even tried to train two circus sea lions as scouts.

Throughout the war, as submarines improved, technology evolved to fight them. Although mines sank relatively few submarines during the war, depth charges, invented in England in 1915, were more promising. These explosive canisters sank and exploded when they reached a desired depth. Accurately dropped from a surface ship, they could cripple or sink a submerged submarine. First, though, the ship had to find the submarine. When a submarine is beneath the surface, sound is the best clue to its presence. Near the end of the war, the British experimented with hydrophones, waterproof microphones that could be dragged through the water to pick up submarine sounds. Because the hydrophones had a tendency to pick up noise from the tow vessels, their

THE ALLIES USED UNDERWATER MICROPHONES CALLED HYDROPHONES TO PICK UP SOUNDS FROM LURKING ENEMY SUB-
MARINES. ONCE A SUB WAS LOCATED, SURFACE DESTROYERS WOULD DROP DEPTH CHARGES.

usefulness at sea was limited. Then, in 1917, the British began testing a
new device called asdic, which didn't just listen for submarine noise but
sent out its own sound wave through the water. The echoes that
bounced back gave a sonic "picture" of objects in the surrounding area.
By the 1930s this technology was developing into sound *na*vigation and
*r*anging, or sonar, which uses high- and low-frequency sound waves to
scan for underwater craft, navigation hazards, and even fish.

By the autumn of 1918 Germany had no choice but to surrender. Its
submarine force, however, fought to the end. On the last day of the war,
a U-boat sank the *Ascot,* a British minesweeper. In all, Germany had destroyed 12.6 million tons (11.4 metric tons) of merchant shipping, 88
percent of it with U-boat attacks and 12 percent with mines and surface
warships. The success of the U-boat fleet owed much to a handful of especially brave, skillful, and lucky officers—60 percent of the damage

done by U-boats was credited to just twenty-two of Germany's four hundred submarine commanders. And although the submarine had not won the war for Germany, it had proved itself as a naval weapon that would be an essential part of any future war at sea.

In the years after the war, both Great Britain and the United States built up fleets of new submarines. Britain focused on medium-sized patrol submarines for use in the North Sea, close to home, and large long-range subs for missions as far away as the Pacific Ocean. Its S-class subs, for example, ranged up to 217 feet (66 meters) in length, with a crew numbering between thirty-eight and forty-nine. The United States also built large submarines that could carry enough fuel and weaponry to operate at great distances from their home ports. Its *Sargo*-class boats measured 310.5 feet (99.6 meters) and carried between fifty and fifty-five crew. The plan for using these submarines in combat was that they would remain submerged during daylight hours to avoid being spotted by airplanes, which had proved during World War I that they could be effective in reconnaissance and battle. At night the subs would surface to take in fresh air, recharge their batteries by running their engines, and cook hot meals for the crew. Some new submarine designs tried to incorporate the airplane. These aircraft-carrying submarines could launch and recover one or more small seaplanes used for reconnaissance missions.

American and British submarine designers also worked on emergency equipment. World War I had seen several extraordinary escapes from sunken submarines. When the *UB-57*, a small German coastal sub, sank in 128 feet (39 meters) of water, its commander did just what Wilhelm Bauer had done years earlier in the *Brandtaucher*—he waited for hours as the sea leaked into the sub, until the pressure inside equalled that outside. During this time, two of the other survivors shot themselves, unable to bear the painful earaches caused by the depth, the difficult breathing, and the anxiety. Finally, the remaining men were able to open the hatch. They rose to the surface, although some of them died of ruptured lungs during the ascent. After ninety minutes afloat in cold

THIS ILLUSTRATION'S ORIGINAL CAPTION READ, "ESCAPING FROM A CRIPPLED SUB IS EASY WHEN YOU KNOW HOW: YOU SIMPLY LIFT THE CONVENIENT MANHOLE COVER, DISREGARD THE WATER PRESSURE, AND AWAY YOU GO!" IF A SUB HAPPENED TO BE CRIPPLED IN SHALLOW WATER, THESE OPTIMISTIC INSTRUCTIONS MIGHT APPLY, BUT SUBMARINE ESCAPES IN DEEP WATER REQUIRED SAFETY EQUIPMENT.

water, those still alive were taken aboard a surface ship.

Another escape involved the *E11,* a British submarine that sank in 45 feet (13.7 meters) of water after being accidentally struck by another British submarine. Again, a few crewmen, trapped in pockets of air, managed to get out of the ship and up to the surface. On several other occasions during the war, sunken submariners were rescued from above by salvage vessels, which hauled the boats high enough above the waterline that the men could get out. Such incidents prompted the development of escape gear for submariners and of rescue equipment designed specially to aid distressed submarines—although neither escape nor rescue would be easy during wartime. British designer Robert H. Davis developed the Davis submarine escape apparatus (DSEA), a buoyancy vest that controlled the wearer's ascent to the surface and came with a thirty-minute supply of oxygen.

Two American naval officers also made important contributions to submarine safety. Charles "Swede" Momsen's assignment was to produce a piece of equipment that would let an individual rise safely from a stricken sub to the surface. The idea was that a sub would carry one of these safety devices for everyone aboard. His 1929 creation, the Momsen lung, was something like a combination of a gas mask and a life jacket. It had breathing tubes for inhaling and exhaling, but before it could be used, it had to be filled with oxygen from a tank near the sub's escape hatch. Around the same time, American officer Allan McCann created a pressurized diving bell that could be carried by ship to the site of a submarine disaster and then lowered to the distressed submarine on a wire—once a diver had secured the wire to the submarine. An air hose would also travel down to supply fresh air to the sub. The McCann bell's two operators would clamp the bell to the sub's escape hatch, half a dozen or so men would enter, and the bell would return them to the surface, repeating the process as often as necessary.

The Momsen lung or DSEA and the McCann bell represented two different approaches to survival in submarine disasters. The Americans favored rescue, while the British favored escape. These different approaches were dramatically tested in 1939. The U.S. submarine *Squalus* sank in 240 feet (73.2 meters) of water off the east coast of the United States, and thirty-three crewmen survived the initial flooding. A McCann bell was rushed to the site. Thirty-five hours after the sinking, the last survivors were removed from the sub. It was a stunning success, but it had been carried out in almost ideal conditions: the bell was not too far away, the weather was good, and the sub was upright on the bottom. Things went differently a week later, when the British sub *Thetis* sank in 150 feet (45.5 meters) of water in Liverpool Bay after water from flooded torpedo tubes entered several compartments in the bow. The boat was overcrowded with 103 people, many of them civilian observers entirely lacking in DSEA training. For hours, while the trapped air grew poisonous with carbon dioxide, the crew focused on efforts to save the vessel and its civilian passengers rather than on escape. A rescue ship arrived the following day but proved unable to cut through the stern of the *Thetis*. The crew began evacuating the sunken craft, but the escape hatch flooded and became unusable. In all, only

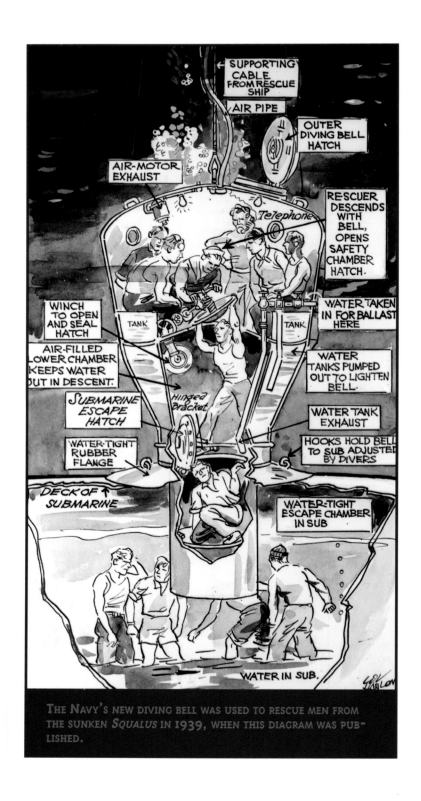

THE NAVY'S NEW DIVING BELL WAS USED TO RESCUE MEN FROM THE SUNKEN *SQUALUS* IN 1939, WHEN THIS DIAGRAM WAS PUBLISHED.

four men escaped the *Thetis* employing DSEA equipment.

In the mid-1930s Germany shook off its defeat and began rebuilding its submarine fleet. The workhorse of its new underwater navy was the Type VII U-boat, similar in size to the British S-class sub. Japan, which was becoming an industrial power, announced its presence on the world stage with a newly expanded navy that included three types of large, long-range submarines and a variety of midget submarines, which were basically battery-driven torpedo launch platforms to be operated by one or two men. Other countries, including Italy and Great Britain, were also experimenting with midget subs. These miniature undersea craft could be used in stealth attacks within harbors and on other covert missions to places that were difficult or impossible for larger submarines to reach.

Submarine development in the 1920s and 1930s drew on the main lesson from World War I: Submarines have a part to play in attacking surface warships, but they are most useful when employed against enemy commerce in enemy waters. By the 1940s, when World War II raged in Europe and the Pacific, the two sides in that global conflict went to war with a new generation of submarines.

AN AMERICAN MERCHANT SHIP SINKS, WATCHED BY GERMAN SUBMARINERS FROM THE CONNING TOWER OF THE U-BOAT THAT FIRED ON IT. SUBMARINES ON BOTH SIDES ATTACKED COMMERCIAL SHIPPING IN WORLD WAR II, WHICH RAGED IN THE PACIFIC AS WELL AS THE ATLANTIC.

World War II and the Nuclear Age

The second world war of the twentieth century began in 1939. In some ways, it was a repeat of the first. Once again Germany was pitted against Great Britain. Germany and its allies were collectively known as the Axis powers; Great Britain and its allies—chiefly France and, after the bombing of Pearl Harbor in December 1941, the United States—were the Allied forces. Once again navies deployed submarines for battle, reconnaissance, and raiding commercial vessels. Once again Germany used its U-boats to attack British merchant shipping, hoping to starve the island nation into submission. As in World War I, the submarine was not the deciding factor in the outcome of the war, but it played an important role.

Each nation used submarines both for attacking commercial vessels and in naval battles. The balance of uses, though, was different for each nation. Germany, which started the war with just fifty-seven submarines but built more than a thousand before the end of the conflict, concentrated on attacking merchant ships and supply lines. Great Britain's chief goal for its submarines was destroying Germany's big, costly surface warships. Japan directed its submarines toward large-scale battles and did not treat commerce raiding as a priority. Late in the war, Japan used submarines to carry supplies to island outposts. The United States also used its subs in fleet engagements and for covert missions such as carrying supplies, photographing enemy harbors, and landing small groups of troops for sabotage operations. The most important role of American submarines, though, was sinking Japanese merchant ships in the Pacific.

The first phase of the submarine war was the Battle of the Atlantic, a years-long struggle between convoys and U-boats. As convoys of merchant ships worked their way across the Atlantic from Canada and the United States toward Great Britain, U-boats waited to attack. Convoys were better protected than in World War I, however. They had help from sub spotters in airplanes, and they had asdic (the British did not adopt the term *sonar* until 1948), which didn't work as well as the Royal Navy had hoped, but did help. They also had radar, a new imaging technology that made it possible to spot U-boats on the surface at night.

But the U-boats also had new advantages as well. Their radio communication had improved, and they had an "unbreakable" code created by a machine called Enigma. This code let U-boat commanders coordinate their movements by radio without fear of being understood—until British code-breakers cracked it, after the Allies captured a German submarine carrying a code machine. Beginning in June 1940, the U-boats also had convenient new home ports on the coast of France, which had fallen under German control. Reaching the Atlantic from France rather than by passing through the dangerous North Sea saved the U-boats

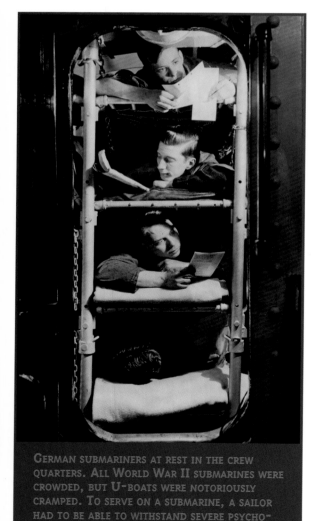

GERMAN SUBMARINERS AT REST IN THE CREW QUARTERS. ALL WORLD WAR II SUBMARINES WERE CROWDED, BUT U-BOATS WERE NOTORIOUSLY CRAMPED. TO SERVE ON A SUBMARINE, A SAILOR HAD TO BE ABLE TO WITHSTAND SEVERE PSYCHOLOGICAL STRESS.

much time, fuel, and risk. The German submarine fleet was ready to try a new tactic devised by Admiral Karl Dönitz: the wolf pack.

A wolf pack could consist of as many as twenty U-boats spread over a fairly wide area. They patrolled individually, looking for convoys. When a U-boat commander found a convoy, he did not attack at once. He radioed the convoy's location to an operations control station in France and then stalked his target, waiting for other U-boats to join him. U-boats typically attacked at night, from the surface, in groups of four to nine. Because they were quicker on the surface than most merchant ships, they could dart in and out of the convoys, exacting severe damage. Facing multiple, fast-moving targets, the escort ships could become disorganized and inefficient. And even if the escorts sank one or more U-boats, others would continue their deadly work.

German submariners later called this early phase of the Battle of the Atlantic "the happy time." Although some U-boats and their crews were lost, the German subs were ripping Allied shipping to shreds. Once the United States had entered the war, the wolf packs moved to new hunting grounds in the western Atlantic, off the east coast of North America, and preyed on shipping there. According to submarine historian Jeffrey Tall, in the first half of 1942, before the United States belatedly adopted the convoy system for its coastal shipping, Germany sank more than six hundred ships in the western Atlantic, losing only eleven U-boats in the process.

As the Battle of the Atlantic wore on, the Allies responded to the challenge of the wolf packs. They used bigger convoys, with more and bigger escorts. To increase air cover in open stretches of ocean, they developed longer-range aircraft and planes that used ships as landing platforms. They made technical improvements to depth charges and torpedoes; they improved radar and experimented with magnetic submarine detectors; and they began targeting the waters around French U-boat bases with air and sea attacks. The Germans made changes, too. In early 1943 they began equipping U-boats with a Dutch invention called the *schnorkel,* or snorkel—a tube that carried air from the sur-

BRITISH DIVERS STEER A MINIATURE SUBMARINE THAT IS REALLY A LARGE TORPEDO MANEUVERED BY ITS CREW, WHICH WOULD SWIM CLEAR BEFORE THE EXPLOSION. SOME WORLD WAR II MINISUBS WERE LITTLE MORE THAN GUIDED MISSILES; OTHERS WERE SMALL VERSIONS OF COMPLETE SUBMARINES.

face to the subs' diesel engines, which needed air to work. This let a submerged U-boat run on engine power, rather than the slower battery power. Despite this new German advantage, however, the Allies' tactics began to pay off. By May 1943, the number of merchant ships falling to U-boats was dropping sharply, while the number of U-boats lost to Allied attack was on the rise. When Germany started losing U-boats faster than it could replace them, Dönitz withdrew his U-boat fleet, and the Battle of the Atlantic was over. U-boats continued to attack Allied shipping from time to time, but the Allies had survived the grave threat to their commercial interests.

Great Britain used its submarines effectively in the Mediterranean Sea, sandwiched between Axis forces in southern Europe and North Africa. British subs attacked shipping with a high rate of success. By cutting off shipments of fuel and other supplies to Erwin Rommel, the German commander in North Africa, the British boats played a key part in securing the Allied victory in the Mediterranean. After Germany attacked Russia in 1941, British submarines also took on the grueling task of escorting convoys of supply ships bound for Russia through the icy waters north of Scandinavia. And one of the British submarine service's great coups was using miniature subs called X-boats to plant crippling explosives near the big German battleship *Tirpitz* as it rested in a Norwegian fjord.

The other main theater of naval combat in World War II was the Pacific, where the United States and Japan had huge fleets with large submarine forces. American subs saw their first major action of the war during Japan's invasion of the Philippines, when they discovered, to their dismay, that their torpedoes did not work properly. For the first year and a half of the war, in fact, American torpedoes caused many problems by exploding too soon or not at all. By mid-1943, however, the main problems had been solved and U.S. subs were equipped with better torpedoes, as well as with radar. The American submarines went on to take part in a number of significant battles. One of their key achievements was sinking two of three Japanese aircraft carriers in the Battle of Leyte Gulf in the Philippines in 1944. But although American sub-

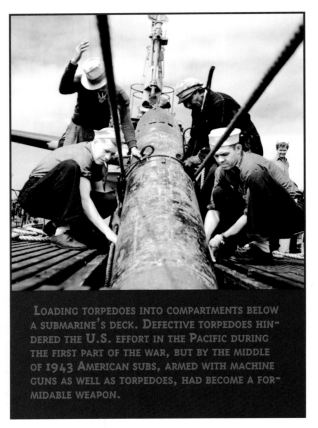

LOADING TORPEDOES INTO COMPARTMENTS BELOW A SUBMARINE'S DECK. DEFECTIVE TORPEDOES HINDERED THE U.S. EFFORT IN THE PACIFIC DURING THE FIRST PART OF THE WAR, BUT BY THE MIDDLE OF 1943 AMERICAN SUBS, ARMED WITH MACHINE GUNS AS WELL AS TORPEDOES, HAD BECOME A FORMIDABLE WEAPON.

marines destroyed 127 Japanese warships in the Pacific theater, their biggest contribution was sinking Japan's merchant fleet.

U.S. subs adopted the wolf-pack approach, although they usually attacked in packs of just three boats. In 1944 alone, American wolf packs sank 603 ships. In fact, the United States did what Germany had twice failed to do—it destroyed a nation's economy and its war effort by cutting its supply lines, almost entirely through the use of submarines. The Japanese turned to deperate measures, including miniature submarines that were little more than suicide torpedoes intended to explode when driven into a ship's hull, but nothing could reverse the course of the war. With its fleet all but useless and its supply of oil and other vital imports cut off, Japan was defeated at sea even before the United States dropped its atomic bombs on the Japanese cities of Hiroshima and Nagasaki in 1945.

Those bombs did more than bring the war to a speedy end. They also marked the beginning of the nuclear age, in which a new source of power would be harnessed for both peaceful and military uses. A decade after the war, nuclear power had revolutionized the submarine. Even before the introduction of the nuclear submarine, however, designers made other important innovations in the postwar years.

One surprising new development involved hull shape. At the time, the preferred shape for submarines was long, thin, and sleek. But American naval researchers, looking for the hull that would offer the best combination of high underwater speed with stability and control, found that the ideal shape was fatter and tube shaped. In 1953 the navy tested the shape with the 204-foot (62.2-meter) *Albacore,* which performed extremely well at high speeds. During the second half of the century, the new hull shape gradually became standard for fast boats. Designers also replaced the old conning towers, some of which were quite large, with smaller deck structures called sails. Like the conning tower, the sail houses an upper command center. It also houses the submarine's various masts, including periscopes, snorkels, radio antennas, and cameras. Because sails interfere with the hydrodynamic properties of hulls, designers attempted to make them as narrow and short as possible.

Navigation also improved. To get around, a submarine needs two navigation systems, one for use on the surface and one for use below. On the surface, a submariner can navigate as if on a conventional surface ship, whether by eyesight, compass and sextant, radio, or—as is

THE *ALBACORE* IS LAUNCHED ON THE NEW ENGLAND COAST, MARCH 25, 1945. WITH A SHORTER, FATTER HULL THAN EARLIER SUBMARINE DESIGNS, THE *ALBACORE* SET NEW SPEED RECORDS. ITS HULL SHAPE WAS EVENTUALLY WIDELY COPIED.

Parts of a Modern Submarine

The inventors and designers of early submarines borrowed many traditional terms from the vocabulary of surface ships. The front of a sub, for example, is the bow, and the rear is the stern. A submarine's outer shell, like the outer shell of any surface ship or boat, is called the hull.

The builders of early underwater boats such as the *Turtle* experimented with a variety of hull shapes. All modern submarines, however, are cigar shaped, although designers are still making refinements to that basic shape as new hydrodynamic research shows them how to make submarines move through water with greater speed and maneuverability. Modern submarines also have double hulls so that they can withstand the pressure of water at depths of 2,000 feet (606 meters). Sandwiched between the two layers of outer and inner hulls are compartments that hold seawater, which is a submarine's ballast.

Submarines have four general systems: life support, propulsion, navcomm, and weapons. The life-support system includes equipment to provide clean air and water, as well food storage, the galley (kitchen), crew quarters, and safety gear. Large modern submarines, whose crews may be at sea for several months at a stretch, even have facilities for watching movies and playing videogames.

This submarine's propulsion source is nuclear. A heavily shielded nuclear reactor produces hot water, which heats water in a set of pipes to the boiling point, producing steam. The steam powers turbine engines that are attached to a propeller at the sub's stern. The spinning propeller drives the sub forward or, when reversed, backward. Four movable diving planes are located near the propeller. Two others stick out from the sail that rises from the upper deck. These planes are adjusted to control the angle of the submarine's movement up, down, or to either side.

A submarine's navcomm system includes the navigation and communications equipment. The sail contains key elements of this system, such as antennas. It also houses the periscope, which has evolved from a simple viewing tube with a mirror into a piece of high-tech electronic gadgetry that incorporates imaging sensors and several kinds of cameras. The sonar dome in the sub's bow is another important navigational tool. Sonar not only "reads" the sea bottom but also scans for objects such as whales, uncharted reefs and other hazards, and other submarines.

Weapons systems have come a long way since the seventeenth-century Rotterdam boat's wooden ram. Nuclear submarines are armed with torpedoes and ballistic missiles. The torpedoes can be fired at submarines or surface ships, while the missiles can be launched at targets on land at ranges of several thousand miles (or kilometers). Hundreds of years ago, thinkers such as Leonardo da Vinci and William Bourne imagined the military potential of an undersea boat. Today's far-ranging, deep-diving, swift subs have turned potential into reality.

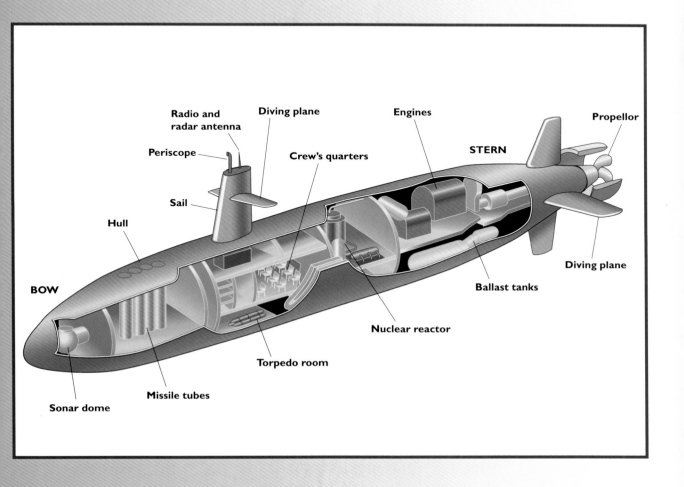

Radio and
radar antenna

Diving plane

Engines

Propellor

Periscope

Crew's quarters

STERN

Sail

Hull

BOW

Diving plane

Ballast tanks

Nuclear reactor

Torpedo room

Sonar dome

Missile tubes

the case today—computers linked to a global positioning system (GPS). None of these methods can be used underwater, however. Starting in the 1950s, engineers devoted much effort to finding a way for a submarine to pinpoint its position while submerged. The result was the ship's inertial navigation system (SINS). This technology is based on gyroscopes that respond to and record movements. Starting from a known location, SINS can accurately track a submarine's movements for about 150 hours of navigation. It must then be reset, which means checking it against an accurate navigational reading from another source.

Sonar is another navigational tool vital to the submerged boat. There are two kinds of sonar, active and passive. Passive sonar detects for sounds generated outside the submarine, such as the sound of another craft's engines. Active sonar requires broadcasting a sound wave, called a ping, that bounces back from objects on the seafloor or in the vicinity. Although active sonar is extremely useful for navigation, its drawback is that a submarine that sends out a ping is, in effect, alerting anyone who happens to be listening to its presence. When stealth is required, subs rely on passive sonar, sometimes towing their sonar equipment behind them to avoid picking up their own sounds. Computerized programs analyze the results of passive sonar scans, providing a complex picture of the environment around the sub and the movements of any potential targets.

Submarines are not as easy to spot by active sonar as they used to be—many of today's subs are covered with rubber coatings designed not to produce sonar echoes. Another technique to make submarines quieter, and therefore less likely to be detected by passive sonar, is rafting. This is a design in which a submarine's noisy equipment is attached to a rigid platform, or raft, which hangs from the internal frame of the submarine. Noise generated by the equipment is absorbed by the raft and the suspension system, so that little of it passes through the hull. In addition, in recent years a few submarines have been built without propellers. They are driven forward by pumped jets of water, which are quieter than propellers.

Making your own submarines quiet is only half the challenge. The other half is listening for other people's subs. In the 1950s the U.S. Navy began building an undersea network of hydrophones to "listen" to ship and submarine traffic. This evolved into the *sound surveillance system* (SOSUS), first along the Atlantic coast of the United States and then later along the Pacific coast and around Hawaii. Today SOSUS consists of undersea sensors linked to onshore processing stations. It is part of a larger network called an integrated undersea surveillance system (IUSS). Although this ocean-monitoring network is sometimes used for scientific research, such as studying undersea earthquakes or tracking whale migrations, its

BRITAIN'S NAVAL DESIGNERS DEVELOPED A PRESSURIZED SAFETY SUIT FOR SUBMARINE ESCAPES. ALTHOUGH THE SUIT HAS BEEN UPDATED WITH NEW EQUIPMENT AND MATERIALS MANY TIMES SINCE THIS 1954 VERSION, ITS FUNCTION AND BASIC DESIGN ARE UNCHANGED.

primary purpose is gathering military intelligence about submarine movements. Other nations have developed similar systems.

Safety took a big step forward after the war, too. As early as the late 1940s, the British Royal Navy had developed an escape suit that would supply a submariner with air during an emergency and would also provide insulation from cold. The escape suit of today is a refined version of that early suit, with a self-inflating hood, a built-in life raft, a distress signal, and a homing beacon.

The most important submarine innovations since World War II have involved power sources. Near the end of the war, Germany had been trying to develop an engine that used high-test hydrogen peroxide (HTP)—the same fuel that later blew up the *Kursk*. After the war,

THE *NAUTILUS* ARRIVES IN PORTLAND, ENGLAND, AFTER MAKING THE FIRST SUBMARINE CROSSING FROM THE PACIFIC TO THE ATLANTIC BENEATH THE ICE CAP AT THE NORTH POLE. LAUNCHED FOUR YEARS EARLIER, IN 1954, *NAUTILUS* BROUGHT THE SUBMARINE INTO THE NUCLEAR ERA.

American and British engineers experimented with this device, called the Walter engine, but found it too explosive. Most navies focused instead on improving the diesel propulsion system for faster and quieter performance. Yet every submarine designer knew that steam engines would be more compact and powerful than diesel. For decades, people had known that old-fashioned, conventional steam engines were less than ideal for use in submarines. As a result of World War II's atomic weapons program, however, designers possessed a new way to heat steam: nuclear power. In 1950 the U.S. Congress authorized the Navy to build the first nuclear-powered submarine, or SSN. The result was the *Nautilus,* which went into operation in 1954.

The designers of the *Nautilus* had created a propulsion system that uses energy produced by splitting atoms in radioactive material to heat water inside a nuclear reactor. A set of pipes known as the primary circuit then carries the hot reactor water into a steam generator that contains a second set of pipes, called the secondary circuit. The reactor water does not flow into the secondary circuit, but heat from the water is transfered to the pipes. Although the water in the primary circuit is pressurized to keep it from boiling, the water in the secondary circuit boils, producing steam, which drives a turbine that turns the submarine's propeller and also provides electricity. Because the primary and secondary circuits are completely separate, the reactor water—which may become contaminated with small amounts of radioactive material—never touches the water that is made into steam.

Nautilus was the fastest submarine in the world. A fast diesel submarine could reach a submerged speed of 19 knots (22 miles or 35 kilometers per hour), but it could hold that speed for only an hour or so, until its battery power ran low. *Nautilus* could reach a maximum speed of 25 knots (29 miles or 46 kilometers per hour) for short bursts and maintain an underwater 16 knots (24 miles or 30 kilometers per hour) for days. Later generations of nuclear submarines were faster still.

Speed is not the only advantage of nuclear power. Nuclear generators do not need oxygen to operate, and their reactor fuel rods can be used for years at a stretch. As far as power is concerned, a nuclear sub could remain submerged almost indefinitely. Its only limitation is life support, but life-support technology has improved dramatically since the mid-twentieth century. For water, most modern submarines have distillation plants that produce tens of thousands of gallons a day of freshwater by removing the salts from seawater, of which they have an abundant supply. For air, a submerged submarine can renew its oxygen from as many as three sources: pressurized storage tanks, canisters that release oyxgen as the product of chemical reactions (similar oxygen canisters are used in spacecraft), or electrolysis plants that use electricity from the generator to break down seawater and produce oxygen. An array of dehumidifers, filters, and scrubbers in the air-circulation system removes moisture, carbon dioxide and other gases, and dust from the air. The British inspector who plaintively described the stench aboard the early Holland boats would have no reason to complain about conditions aboard a modern nuclear sub.

The only remaining challenge is food. Because nuclear submarines are rather large—they have to be, to support the heavy shielding needed to protect the crew from radiation coming from the reactor— they typically have sufficient storage space to hold a lot of rations, as the crew of the 447-foot (136.2-meter), nuclear-powered USS *Triton* proved in 1960, when they became the first people ever to travel around the world submerged. Speaking later about this historic eighty-four-day journey, which covered 36,014 miles (57,959 kilometers), commander Ned Beach said, "We were going to finish that trip if we had to do it rowing the ship with oars." The sub did approach the surface once during its trip around the globe, bringing the top of its sail above the water so that a sick crewman could be evacuated.

Nuclear power is not without danger. After all, the reactor that drives a submarine uses the same materials and laws of physics as the bombs that leveled Hiroshima and Nagasaki. Although reactors are designed with safety as the first concern, some critics fear that certain types of accidents or attacks might cause a reactor explosion. Environmental concerns about radioactive leaks into the ocean arose after the United States lost two SSNs at sea within five years—*Thresher* in 1963 and *Scorpion* in 1968. Another nuclear submarine, the Russian *K-129,* also went down in 1968; the Central Intelligence Agency of the United States, with the cooperation of billionaire Howard Hughes, mounted a secret operation to salvage and study *K-129,* with limited success. Since that time, the number of nuclear submarines—and the number of nuclear submarine losses—has continued to rise. The safe disposal of spent reactor fuel from the world's nuclear fleets may be an even bigger problem; it is part of the challenge the modern world faces in handling nuclear waste.

In 1949, five years before *Nautilus* entered the U.S. Navy, the Soviet Union test-fired its first atomic bomb. Suddenly the world had two superpowers. The Soviet Union and the United States, each with a cluster of allies, faced each other in an uneasy standoff called the cold war. To keep the cold war from breaking out into a conflagration that might easily involve the use of atomic bombs, the superpowers used a strategy called deterrence. Each side had to convince the other that whoever launched the first attack would be attacked in return. Fear of retaliation would prevent, or deter, either side from making the first strike. By the late 1950s, the principal element of deterrence was the intercontinental ballistic missile (ICBM), a long-range, rocket-propelled, electronically guided explosive that could be fired from a submarine at distant targets on land.

Submarines were superb for deterrence. They were much harder to hit than onshore missile bases because they were smaller and, of course, mobile. In addition, they could get close to the enemy. While both sides in the cold war developed and stockpiled missiles to be launched from ground and air, they also built and deployed submarines armed with banks of missiles.

For a couple of years, the United States had the advantage of being the only nation with a swift, long-range, nuclear-powered submarine. Then, in 1958, the Soviet Union launched its first nuclear sub. For most

WITH THE DEVELOPMENT OF GUIDED MISSILES, SUBMARINES BECAME MOBILE LAUNCH PADS FOR ROCKETS, WHICH COULD BE FIRED EITHER SUBMERGED OR ON THE SURFACE. THESE MISSILES GAVE SUBS THE POWER TO ATTACK DISTANT LAND TARGETS, SUCH AS ENEMY CITIES. THE THREAT OF SUCH ATTACKS, MILITARY PLANNERS FELT, WOULD KEEP ANY NATION FROM LAUNCHING THE FIRST STRIKE.

of the rest of the century, the two superpowers engaged in a submarine arms race. For example, after a Soviet sub surprised the U.S. Navy in 1968 by keeping up with it on high-speed maneuvers, the Navy built a new, faster submarine, the *Los Angeles* class, that entered service in 1976. By the mid-1970s the United States had developed a ballistic missile with a range of more than 4,000 miles (6,437 kilometers), but it was too large for any existing submarine to carry. The navy built the 560-foot (170-meter) *Ohio* class to carry it. Meanwhile, the Soviets were building their own 564-foot (171.3-meter) *Typhoon* class, which was supposed to wait out any nuclear conflict under the Arctic icepack, then break through the ice to launch retaliatory missiles.

Over the second half of the twentieth century, the United States and the Soviet Union continued to create deterrence fleets of large, nuclear-powered submarines carrying both nuclear and nonnuclear warheads. These boats are known as SSBNs—or, in the U.S. Navy, as boomers. Designed for use against land targets from a great distance, they are considered strategic submarines because of their role in long-term military strategy. Great Britain, France, and China have also built their own SSBNs.

During the same period, these nations and others also developed smaller, faster submarines for use in reconnaissance (or espionage). Because these submarines were also designed to be used against surface ships or other subs in the event of war, they are called attack or hunter-killer subs. Although boomers are nuclear powered, an attack sub can have either a nuclear or a diesel engine. All of them, however, are quieter, faster, and more capable than the best of the World War II–era submarines they have replaced.

THE LURE OF SUNKEN TREASURE WAS A KEY MOTIVE BEHIND THE DEVELOPMENT
OF THE DIVING BELL, WHICH COULD BE USED TO SALVAGE CARGO FROM COASTAL
WRECKS. SALVAGERS DESCEND IN THE BELL. THE BARREL HOLDS A RESERVE OF
AIR. THE WORKER CAN FASTEN GOODS TO THE X-SHAPED FRAMEWORK TO BE
HAULED TO THE SURFACE.

Bathyscaphes, Submersibles, and Peacetime Pastimes

A submarine is not the only way to get to the bottom of the sea. Back in the sixteenth and seventeenth centuries, while Drebbel and De Son were building the early submarines, other undersea pioneers were creating diving bells. Using these devices, divers could work or explore beneath the surface of the water. Although diving bells were different from submarines and followed a separate line of development, the two technologies eventually merged. Modern versions of the diving bell are also similar to the submarine. Among them are minisubs and submersibles such as *Alvin,* probably the most famous deepocean research vehicle in the world.

Early diving bells were simply that—large bells (or boxes) that were open on the bottom. When lowered straight down into the water, they held a bubble of air trapped inside. The principle of the diving bell is at least as old as Aristotle's description of Alexander the Great beneath the waves at Tyre. The first recorded diving bell, however, was made in 1531 by an Italian named Guglielmo de Lorena, who hoped to use it to salvage some boats that an ancient Roman emperor was supposed to have sunk in a lake. De Lorena did not succeed in this goal, but he showed that the diving bell worked. The next century saw a number of diving-bell demonstrations in Europe. In 1640 a Frenchman named Jean Barrie received royal permission to use his diving bell to salvage wrecks and went on to recover the cargo of a sunken ship. Other successful salvage operations followed, in various locations.

In 1689 Denis Papin, the French mathematician who may have invented an early submarine or two, pointed out that supplying a diving bell with pressurized air pumped through a hose would extend its range of operations. British scientist Edmund Halley quickly put this idea into practice, building a large wooden diving bell with air tubes. He and a few friends friends, Halley later claimed, had spent an hour and a half in the bell in 60 feet (18.3 meters) of water. By the nineteenth century, open diving bells had become fairly elaborate, with lights, ballast systems, and air pumps. Engineers used them when building harbors and bridges.

The next development was the closed bell, or bathysphere. This spherical vessel was lowered on a steel cable from a surface ship. If properly made, it could withstand a considerable amount of water pressure. The bathysphere had no immediate commercial or military purpose—it was designed for scientific exploration. In 1934, in an expedition funded by the New York Zoological Society and the National Geographic Society, a bathysphere less than 5 feet (1.5 meters) across carried two American scientists, Charles William Beebe and Otis Barton, into the sea off the coast of Bermuda, where they peered through a tiny window of thick quartz at the ocean 3,028 feet (923 meters) down. It was the greatest depth anyone had reached—and survived.

Around the same time, a Swiss scientist named Auguste Piccard was exploring the earth's upper atmosphere in a gondola, or passenger compartment, attached to the underside of a huge gas balloon. Piccard was certain that the same technology could be used for undersea exploration. Drawing on what Beebe had learned about bathysphere construction and survival at great depths, he built a series of vessels he called bathyscaphes (from the Greek words for "deep ship"). Like a diving bell or bathysphere, a bathyscaphe was carried to its site of operations on the deck of a ship. But unlike a bell or bathysphere, once it was lowered into the sea it was not connected to the surface but moved freely on its own using a battery-powered electric motor.

THE BATHYSCAPHE *TRIESTE*, SHOWN BEING WINCHED ONTO A TRANSPORT SHIP, MADE THE DEEPEST RECORDED DIVE IN HISTORY IN 1960. ITS TWO PASSENGERS DESCENDED 6.7 MILES (11 KILOMETERS) INTO THE MARIANA TRENCH IN THE PACIFIC OCEAN.

The bathyscaphe had two parts. The upper section corresponded to the gas bag of Piccard's great ballon. Called the float, it resembled a small submarine because it had a flat deck and a tower that contained an entry hatch. In reality it was a large tank for carrying gasoline, which provided buoyancy because it is lighter than water. A ballast of water and iron pellets caused the bathyscaphe to sink; releasing the ballast caused it to rise again. Below the float hung an observation chamber that was much like a bathysphere, equipped with controls for driving the bathyscaphe.

Piccard's last and biggest bathyscaphe was the 59.5-foot (18-meter) *Trieste*, named for the Italian city whose residents, inspired by Piccard's speeches about furthering the cause of science, contributed much of the cost of building it. Launched in 1953, *Trieste* was later bought by the U.S. Navy. In 1960 a navy lieutenant named Don Walsh and Piccard's son, Jacques Piccard, used *Trieste* to make the deepest manned dive on record: 35,800 feet (6.7 miles, or 11 kilometers) down in the deepest part of the world's ocean, the Mariana Trench near Guam in the Pacific.

The bathyscaphe was a submersible, a craft that operates independently underwater, as a submarine does. Unlike a submarine, though, a submersible is not made to operate on the surface. Submersibles are smaller than submarines (except for some midget subs) and are designed for short-range use on limited trips. If a submersible is to be used far from shore, a surface ship or submarine carries it to the dive site and provides support services, such as communication and navigation assistance. Some submersibles remain tethered, or connected, by power and communication lines to their support ships or platforms.

Four years after the *Trieste*'s historic dive, the Woods Hole Oceanographic Institute (WHOI) and the U.S. Navy built the submersible *Alvin,* which carries a pilot and two observers. *Alvin* immediately proved its usefulness by inspecting part of an undersea array of cables and submarine sensors that the Navy was building near the Bahamas. In 1966 *Alvin* made headlines around the world by helping in the recovery of a nuclear bomb that had been lost from an American aircraft off the coast of Spain. *Alvin*'s most famous success came in 1986, when Robert Ballard and other WHOI scientists located the wreck of the passenger liner *Titanic,* which sank in 1912 in 13,000 feet (3,962 meters) of water in the North Atlantic.

Since its launch in 1964 *Alvin* has made more than four thousand dives. Its observation chamber has been replaced several times and is now made of titanium instead of the original aluminum. When new, *Alvin* could operate at depths of up to 6,000 feet (1,829 meters), but now it is operational to 14,000 feet (4,267). The submersible is housed on a support ship called *Atlantis,* which carries it to missions around the world. In recent years *Alvin* has often been used for seafloor mapping and for the study of deep-ocean chemical and thermal vents, places where new life-forms are being discovered.

Alvin may be the best-known submersible in the world, but there are many others. The French submersible *Nautile,* which can operate at nearly 20,000 feet (6,096 meters), removed many items from the wreck of the *Titanic.* The University of Hawaii uses the *Makakai* for geological and biological research in the water around the Hawaiian islands. The 13-foot (4-meter) one-person *Deep Flight,* launched in 1996, was built for use in undersea filming. Its designers, as well as other teams worldwide, hope to mass-produce small submersibles for private ownership. Navies use submersibles, too. Since the 1960s, the small craft have been sent on covert military missions, such as studying lost enemy subs and laying surveillance equipment. Commercial uses have included oil exploration and undersea pipeline construction and inspection. Deep submersible rescue vessels (DSRVs) are specifically designed and equipped to remove people from submarines in trouble.

During undersea operations such as research and rescue, submersibles may need help from supplemental equipment. One such piece of equipment is the armored diving suit, which lets a diver function at depths of up to 2,000 feet (610 meters), if necessary, to perform difficult operations such as attaching a rescue unit to a damaged submarine hatch. Even more useful is the remotely operated vehicle (ROV), which is basically a set of instruments (such as cameras) or tools (such as jointed arms with movable claws) on a motorized platform. An ROV is typically linked to a submersible by control cables and operated by someone in the submersible. The Australian navy, however, has developed a remote-controlled rescue submersible that can be operated from the surface during a submarine rescue.

The newest generation of submersibles is autonomous (independently operating) underwater vehicles, or AUVs; sometimes these are also called unmanned undersea vehicles, or UUVs. As British submariner and historian Jeffrey Tall says in *Submarines & Deep-Sea Vehicles* (2002), "AUVs are ROVs with brains." These self-propelled vehicles, some of them smaller than torpedoes, have been used for such tasks as locating mines and inspecting fiber-optic cable beneath the Arctic icepack, far from any possible supervision by submersible. Equipped with onboard computers, AUVs function by following a prepared set of instructions, or by adapting to circumstances in real time according to programmed variables, or with minimal guidance from

DEEP ROVERS ARE ONE-PERSON SUBMERSIBLES WITH JOINTED ARMS THAT LET THEIR DRIVERS PERFORM UNDERWATER TASKS SUCH AS WELDING. THESE SUBMERSIBLES OPERATE AT DEPTHS OF UP TO 948 FEET (300 METERS).

outside in the form of data received through a cable. Civilian and military scientists are now working to develop smarter, more agile, more capable AUVs. The next generation of these seagoing robots will have a wide variety of possible uses, including oceanographic research, deep-sea mineral exploration, undersea sound monitoring, laying and sweeping mines, and tracking their relatives, submarines.

THE *U32*, FIRST OF A NEW CLASS OF GERMAN STATE-OF-THE-ART SUBMARINES, IS INAUGURATED INTO THE NAVY IN OCTOBER 2005. AT THE DAWN OF THE TWENTY-FIRST CENTURY, NAVIES OF SEVERAL NATIONS INTRODUCED NEW, VERSATILE ALL-PURPOSE UNDERSEA BOATS.

Submarines of the Twenty-first Century

No one knows exactly how many submarines there are in the world in the early years of the twenty-first century. The great majority of them, though, are military submarines. All of the submarines in the American, British, and French navies are nuclear. China and Russia have both nuclear and diesel-electric submarines. India, which leased a Soviet nuclear sub in the 1980s, may be working on a nuclear submarine program of its own. Swedish naval submarines use a form of the Walter engine that runs on liquid oxygen rather than high-test hydrogen peroxide. At least forty other countries, from Algeria to Yugoslavia, have either built or bought diesel-electric submarines for their navies. Some of these boats are old and used seldom or not at all; others have limited ranges of operation. Still, together they make up such a large and varied array of undersea craft that even the boastful Captain Nemo of Jules Verne's *Nautilus* would surely be impressed.

The biggest naval sub fleets are those of the United States and Russia, which inherited most of the former Soviet Union's submarines. When the cold war ended in the late twentieth century, so did the immediate threat of nuclear war between the two superpowers. The role of the submarine in deterrence, however, did not end. Most military planners today still regard the SSBN, the long-range nuclear submarine armed with ballistic missiles, as a strategic necessity. The certainty of retaliation from a ballistic sub may prevent an aggressive power from making the first attack. The threat now is not from Soviet missiles but from weapons of mass destruction—whether chemical, biological, or nuclear—that might be used by any one of a number of nations or political groups.

The ballistic subs used for strategic deterrence cruise around the world, as secretly as possible, and spend much of their time in mid-ocean and in deep water. They are what navies call blue-water craft. But modern subs are also used for intelligence gathering, for landing covert teams, and for attack. These missions take place in brown water—the shallower waters over the continental shelf, close to landmasses. Such activities are carried out by the smaller, faster attack submarines, which now carry torpedoes that can be fired at land targets as well as at other ships. In the 1990s, attack submarines fired Tomahawk missiles with non-nuclear warheads during conflicts in Iraq, Bosnia, and Kosovo.

Intelligence-gathering missions involve reconnaissance, surveillance, or both. Reconnaissance is gathering information about a place. Examples include filming, photographing, and mapping the approaches to beaches where troops may have to land, or harbors that ships may have to enter. Surveillance is watching the movements of ships or other submarines—ideally, without being detected. When the American submarines *Toledo* and *Memphis* shadowed the exercises of the Russian *Kursk* in the Barents Sea in 2000, they were engaging in surveillance.

In the first years of the twenty-first century, the U.S. Navy and the British Royal Navy each introduced a new class of submarine to meet a wide variety of purposes. The British *Astute* class and the American *Virginia* class are designed to be fast, agile, and stealthy enough for brown-water operations, but also to have the endurance and range to perform long blue-water missions if necessary. The 377-foot (115-meter) 134-person *Virginia,* commissioned into the U.S. Navy in 2004, is a state-of-the-art example of this new type of all-purpose sub. It has a photonics mast, which is a remote-controlled unit that includes videocameras, a laser range-finder for sighting on targets, heat imagers, and other high-tech sensors as well as several communications antennas. The *Virginia*'s control room has touch-sensitive computer screens for monitoring and adjusting all of the ship's functions. The sub is steered with a joystick—not too different from the ones used with video-games—which gives better control than the traditional wheel. It is the world's quietest submarine, with a sound-absorbent coating, a control room mounted on springs to prevent sound from traveling into the hull, and decks that are isolated from the hull for the same reason. It carries a variety of weapons for short- and long-range use (although not, at this time, nuclear-armed warheads). Built at a cost of more than $1.65 billion, with three more of its class on their way, the *Virginia* has been called the submarine of the future.

The future, though, can be full of surprises. Some scientists and military planners have speculated about the possible development of a new

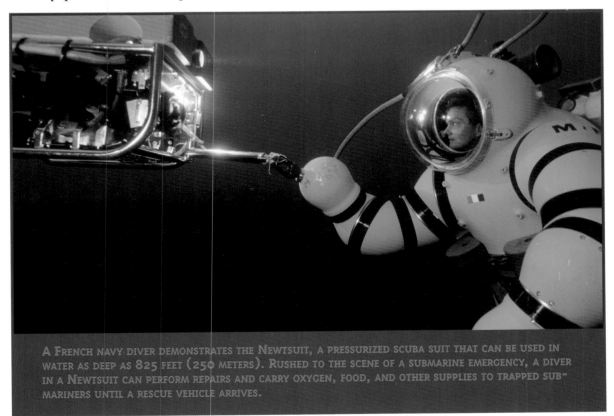

A FRENCH NAVY DIVER DEMONSTRATES THE NEWTSUIT, A PRESSURIZED SCUBA SUIT THAT CAN BE USED IN WATER AS DEEP AS 825 FEET (250 METERS). RUSHED TO THE SCENE OF A SUBMARINE EMERGENCY, A DIVER IN A NEWTSUIT CAN PERFORM REPAIRS AND CARRY OXYGEN, FOOD, AND OTHER SUPPLIES TO TRAPPED SUB-MARINERS UNTIL A RESCUE VEHICLE ARRIVES.

technology that would "see" through water, stripping away the secrecy that is the submarine's unique feature. The breakthrough could come from dramatic improvements in a known technology, such as the computer programs that analyze sounds carried through water, or from an entirely new technology, such as a new kind of aircraft- or satellite-based imaging system. For the present, though, such a breakthrough remains in the realm of science fiction. Submarines will continue to operate. What new forms might the next generations of submarines take?

One trend already under way is the use of ROVs and AUVs to perform tasks that were formerly carried out by submarines. Some submarine analysts think that in the future, submarines will serve mainly as platforms from which unmanned vehicles will operate. A largely automated submarine could operate with a small crew—perhaps, someday, with no crew at all. Other future developments may grow out of some of today's research projects. For example, tests have shown that when a submarine passes through water that has been injected with chemicals called liquid polymers, water resistance is significantly increased, boosting the sub's speed. Submarines may one day be equipped with polymers to spray into the water, as an octopus sprays ink, when they need a burst of speed. One researcher, Dennis Bushnell, a descendant of the David Bushnell who built the Revolutionary War submarine *Turtle,* has even speculated that future submarines might be able to manufacture their own polymers from plankton they harvest.

Advances in drive technology—the means by which the energy from a nuclear sub's steam turbine is transferred to its propeller—could make submarines quieter in the future. The gears that connect a nuclear submarine's steam turbine to its propeller are one of the boat's chief sources of noise. Connecting the turbine to an electric drive rather than to mechanical gears would greatly reduce the noise a sub produces, and engineers are now researching electric drives. Another possibility is a drive system using magnets, with no moving parts at all. Experimental versions of this drive exist, but so far they are not powerful enough to produce the speeds that modern submarines need.

Changes in hull construction would allow submarines to operate at new depths. Submarines today are built of high-strength steel. They can operate safely to about 1,800 feet (548.6 meters). Below that depth, pressure crushes the hull; some submarines cannot even go that deep. The Soviet Union built a titanium-hulled submarine that could dive to 3,000 feet (914.4 meters), but that construction method will probably not be repeated, because titanium is very expensive. Some submarine strategists have proposed experimenting with fiberglass hulls in the hope of building subs that could dive to depths as great as 4,000 or even 8,000 feet (1,129 or 2,438 meters). At such depths, a sub could easily evade attack. It could also use upward-pointing sonar to track the movements of whole fleets. The current military emphasis on brown-water operations, though, means that funds will probably not be devoted to developing deep-diving submarines in the near future.

Midget submarines—used by several nations during World War II—are making a comeback. Iran, North Korea, and Yugoslavia have all built midget submarines. Far less costly than full-sized submarines, these four- to twenty-person craft are carried over long distances by transport ships, then released to perform their missions. They are armed with attack torpedoes and can also be used for such operations as patrols, laying mines, and carrying divers on covert missions.

Tourist submarines are another form of midget sub. Auguste Piccard operated the first tourist submarine in Lake Geneva, Switzerland, in the mid-twentieth century. Today more than fifty small submarines, run as commercial ventures, carry tourists to view such underwater attractions as coral reefs. The largest of these battery-powered submarines can carry more than sixty passengers and descend to about 150 feet (45.7 meters). Although tourist subs operate mostly in clear, fairly shallow water around tropical resorts, some observers expect that recreational submarines or submersibles will one day go much deeper, carrying venturesome tourists into a world that is now known only to submariners and scientists.

Closer to the surface, another trend is catching on: human-powered

The designers of this *Gemini* recreational submersible call it "the world's first underwater sports car."

submarines, or HPS. Like the early submarines, such as David Bushnell's *Turtle* and Robert Fulton's *Nautilus,* modern HPS harness human muscle power to drive a boat underwater. Most are wet subs, which means that they are not watertight; their operators wear scuba gear to breathe underwater. Some of these new HPS are created by independent inventors hoping to produce recreational devices for divers. Others are invented by college and university students as team projects. In the United States and other countries, engineering departments of many schools have introduced programs in which students learn about hydrodynamics, materials, and construction techniques by designing and building human-powered submarines. These HPS are not expected to reach great depths, only to move underwater as fast as possible.

Since 1989 two organizations in the United States have coordinated HPS races for teams from colleges and universities. Entries have ranged from sleek, computer-equipped fiberglass pods to a streamlined suit that is half air bubble, half finned tail like that of a mermaid. Most are operated by pedals and gears, like racing bicycles. Despite the high-tech materials, space-age design, and flashy paint jobs of these new human-powered submarines, Bushnell and Fulton would recognize them at once as descendants of their own creations, some of the first boats ever to travel under the waves instead of on them.

asdic—An early form of sonar, developed by the British during World War II.

AUV—Autonomous underwater vehicle, a self-guided, self-propelled drone that carries out preprogrammed tasks.

ballast—Material carried to give a submarine enough weight to sink; modern submarines use seawater as ballast, adding and releasing it as necessary to sink or rise.

bathyscaphe—A steerable submersible vessel for manned deep-sea exploration; usually a sealed observation cabin attached to a tank whose pressure can be adjusted to rise or sink.

bathysphere—A nonsteerable, spherical vessel for deep-sea observation, usually lowered from a ship by a cable.

blockade—Strategy of keeping an enemy from receiving help or supplies by preventing ships from reaching its harbor through the use of patrols, mines, submarines, or other means.

blow—Emergency surfacing maneuver that involves expelling ballast rapidly from the submarine to lighten it.

buoyancy—The tendency of an object to float in fluid; negative buoyancy means that it sinks.

conning tower—The structure on a submarine's deck; usually contains an entrance to the submarine as well as navigation and communication gear; located above the control room and can be used as command center on the surface; replaced in modern submarines with a more compact structure called a sail.

hydrophone—Device for detecting sound waves underwater.

mine—Floating bomb or explosive device that can damage shipping; minelayers are boats that place mines in the sea, and minesweepers are boats that try to collect them safely.

reconnaissance—Gathering information about a place, usually in advance of a planned operation.

ROV—Remotely operated vehicle, an unmanned undersea craft equipped with cameras or other sensors and controlled by operators on the surface; used for specialized purposes such as marine research, salvage, oil exploration, removel of mines, and inspection of undersea oil pipelines and other structures.

sonar—From *sound navigation and ranging*, a system that uses sound waves and their reflections off objects to locate those objects; developed to detect and locate submarines.

submarine—Vessel that operates independently both on and below the surface; modern submarines are designed primarily for underwater use.

submersible—Vessel that operates independently underwater but is smaller than a submarine; designed for use in a limited area for a short time, usually carried by ship to and from the site of operations.

surveillance—Watching the movements of a subject (such as a ship or submarine) without being seen in turn.

ton—Used as a measure of a vessel's volume; refers to the volume of water it displaces.

torpedo—A bomb or other explosive that can travel through the water to its target; since the late nineteenth century, torpedoes have been self propelled.

1580
Englishman William Bourne publishes a brief description of an under-water vessel.

about 1620
Cornelis Drebbel, a Dutch inventor working in England, builds the first working underwater boat.

1776
American David Bushnell's *Turtle* is the first submarine to attack an enemy ship.

1800
American inventor Robert Fulton, working in France, builds and successfully tests the *Nautilus*.

1850s
German officer Wilhelm Bauer builds working submarines for Germany and Russia.

1862
The U.S. Navy's first submarine, the *Alligator,* enters service; it sinks the next year.

1864
The Confederate States' *H. L. Hunley* is the first submarine to sink an enemy warship (the U.S. Navy's *Housatonic*); the *Hunley* also sinks, not to be found until 1995.

1867–1869
British inventor Robert Whitehead develops the self-propelled mine, or torpedo, which becomes the submarine's main weapon.

1870
French author Jules Verne's novel *Twenty Thousand Leagues under the Sea* introduces Captain Nemo and his sub, the *Nautilus,* to a world-wide audience.

1874
New Jersey teacher John P. Holland begins designing submarines.

1879
British clergyman George Garrett builds the *Resurgam,* the world's first powered submarine, which has a steam engine; it sinks while being towed.

1881
John P. Holland launches the *Fenian Ram,* built for Irish revolutionaries to use against the British navy; it is tested in New York City but never used.

1880s
Inventors of many nations experiment with submarine design; several navies build or buy submarines; France leads submarine development.

1900
John P. Holland's sixth submarine is bought by the U.S. Navy; the "Holland boat," with a gasoline engine, is widely copied, launching the age of the submarine.

1906
Germany launches its first U-boat.

1910s
Diesel engines begin to replace gasoline engines on submarines.

1914–1918
During World War I, German U-boats wreak havoc on merchant ships carrying supplies to Great Britain; navies develop depth charges, convoys, and asdic as anti-submarine measures.

1915
A German U-boat sinks the passenger liner *Lusitania,* sparking new debates about the morality of submarine warfare. ·

1939
When the USS *Squalus* sinks in 240 feet (73.2 meters) of water, a newly developed submarine rescue device saves thirty-three crewmen; the *Thetis* disaster leads the British to improve their own escape system.

1939–1945
During World War II, German U-boats in "wolf pack" formation harass shipping routes; submarine warfare occurs in the Atlantic and Pacific oceans and the Mediterranean Sea.

1955
The USS *Nautilus,* the world's first nuclear-powered submarine, enters the navy.

1960
The USS *Triton* is the first submarine to sail around the world underwater, covering 36,014 (57,959 kilometers) miles in eight-four days.

1963
The American nuclear submarine *Thresher* sinks.

1968
The United States loses its second nuclear sub, the *Scorpion.*

2000
The Russian submarine *Kursk* sinks in the Barents Sea, and survivors perish before they can be rescued; the U.S. Navy celebrates the one hundredth anniversary of its submarine fleet.

2001
While practicing an emergency ascent, the U.S. submarine *Greeneville* sinks the Japanese vessel *Ehime Maru.*

2004
The U.S. Navy commissions the 377-foot (115-meter) *Virginia,* first in a new series of submarines designed for covert missions as well as warfare; underwater explorers search for the wreckage of the Civil War–era *Alligator.*

2005
An international effort rescues survivors from the sunken Russian mini-sub *Priz;* the U.S. Navy sub *San Francisco* crashes into an undersea mountain.

Web Sites

These are some of the most useful Web sites about submarines. Many other sites also provide information on the subject.

U.S. Navy—The Submarine
www.navy.mil/palib/ships/submarines.html
The U.S. Navy's information page about submarines has links to several Navy sites, including fact sheets about attack and ballistic-missile submarines.

Submarine Technology through the Years
www.chinfo.navy.mil/navpalib/ships/submarines/centennial/subhistory.html
Part of the U.S. Navy's Submarine Centennial, this site offers illustrations and brief descriptions of milestones in American submarine development.

About Submarines
http://inventors.about.com/library/inventors/blsubmarine.htm
A concise overview of the history of submarine design and the use of submarines in war, with links to other resources, including a list of submarines that are now in museums or public attractions.

Submarine History
www.submarine-history.com/NOVAone/html
Created for the television series *NOVA* by Brayton Harris, retired navy
captain and author of *The Navy Times Book of Submarines,* this site is
a good, fairly detailed time line of international submarine history, both
technical development and use in war.

Submarines, Secrets, and Spies
www.pbs.org/wgbh/nova/subsecrets.html
This companion site to the 1999 *NOVA* show "Submarines, Secrets,
and Spies" features virtual tours through submarines and a section on
day-to-day life in a sub.

How Submarines Work
www.science.howstuffworks.com/submarine.htm
Good introduction to the technology of submarines, with sections on
diving and surfacing, life support, power supply, navigation, and rescue,
as well as links to other resources.

Bibliography

FOR STUDENTS

DiMercurio, Michael and Michael Benson. *The Complete Idiot's Guide to Submarines.* New York: Alpha Books, 2003.

Mallard, Neil. *Submarine.* New York: DK Publishing, 2003.

Payan, Gregory and Alexander Guelke. *Life on a Submarine.* New York: Children's Press, 2000.

Preston, Diana. *Remember the Lusitania.* New York: Walker and Co., 2003.

Walker, Sally M. *Secrets of a Civil War Submarine: Solving the Mysteries of the* H. L. Hunley. Minneapolis: Carolrhoda Books, 2005.

Woodford, Chris. *Ships and Submarines.* New York: Facts on File, 2004.

FOR TEACHERS OR ADVANCED READERS

Clancy, Tom. *Submarine: A Guided Tour inside a Nuclear Warship.* New York: Berkeley Books, 1993.

Dunmore, Spencer. *Lost Subs: From the* Hunley *to the* Kursk, *the Greatest Submarines Ever Lost—and Found.* Cambridge, MA: Da Capo, 2002.

Flynn, Ramsey. *Cry from the Deep: The Submarine Disaster that Riveted the World and Put the New Russia to the Ultimate Test.* New York: HarperCollins, 2004.

Gunton, Michael. *Submarines at War: A History of Undersea Warfare from the American Revolution to the Cold War.* New York: Carroll and Graf, 2003.

Harris, Brayton. *The Navy Times Book of Submarines: A Political, Social, and Military History.* New York: Berkeley Books, 1997.

Hicks, Brian. *Raising the* Hunley: *The Remarkable History and Recovery of the Lost Confederate Submarine.* New York: Ballantine Books, 2002.

Hutchinson, Robert. *Jane's Submarines: War beneath the Waves from 1776 to the Present Day.* New York: HarperCollins, 2001.

Kemp, Paul. *Underwater Warriors: The Fighting History of Midget Submarines.* London: Cassell, 2000. Originally published 1996.

Lawliss, Chuck. *The Submarine Book.* Short Hills, NJ: Burford Books, 2000.

Parrish, Thomas. *The Submarine: A History.* New York: Viking, 2004.

Preston, Antony. *Submarine Warfare: An Illustrated History.* San Diego, CA: Thunder Bay Press, 1999.

Stern, Robert C. *Battle beneath the Waves: U-Boats at War.* London: Cassell, 2002. Originally published 1999.

Tall, Jeffrey. *Submarines & Deep-Sea Vehicles.* San Diego, CA: Thunder Bay Press, 2002.

Index

Page numbers for illustrations are in **boldface**.

About the Author

Rebecca Stefoff has written numerous nonfiction books for readers of all ages. Her works include biographies of historical and literary figures as well as books about science, nature, and exploration. Stefoff is the author of *The Telephone* in the Great Inventions series. She has also written about discoveries and their effects in such works as *Charles Darwin and the Evolution Revolution* (Oxford University Press, 1996). Among her other works are the ten-volume Benchmark Books series North American Historical Atlases and the five-volume World Historical Atlases series. You can find more information about Stefoff and her books for young readers at her Web site, www.rebeccastefoff.com.